Sleeping Beauty

by

Matt Beames

AURORA METRO BOOKS

To my son, Oli

And to Dan and Dave and The Point Youth Theatre,
with thanks

Matt Beames

Matt Beames is a writer based in the Southampton area, and is the Associate Writer of The Berry Theatre in Hedge End. He loves stories of all kinds and has been writing and telling his own since childhood. His work is often inspired by and draws on folklore and mythology from around the world.

Matt writes for the theatre as well as long and short fiction, poetry and also comic books. His writing for theatre includes more than ten plays and adaptations that have been performed in various professional and youth theatre productions in the UK and even as far as Seattle, USA.

www.mattbeames.co.uk

@MattBeames

First published in the UK in 2017 by Aurora Metro Publications Ltd.

67 Grove Avenue, Twickenham, TW1 4HX

www.aurorametro.com   info@aurorametro.com

Production: Simon Smith

With many thanks to: Marina Tuffier, Abi Silverthorne, Ana Rice-Wallace, Harry Read, Josh Patterson, Mary Boland and Madeleine Cuckson.

Printed in the UK by 4edge Limited.

ISBNs:

978-1-912430-05-5 (print)

978-1-912430-06-2 (ebook)

CONTENTS

The Point Youth Theatre (PYT) is an open access company for young people aged 5–21 giving everyone the opportunity to take part in safe, empowering and challenging theatre regardless of age, background or ability.

PYT operates an ensemble approach to everything they do, putting young people in the driving seat, creating equality and camaraderie within the youth theatre. They provide inspirational, engaging and celebratory events that allow young people the opportunity to express themselves, develop a passion and make the most of their talent.

Through collaboration between youth theatre members and creative professionals, PYT creates exciting, honest and enjoyable productions that stimulate and challenge participants and audiences alike.

As well as weekly workshops PYT offer a range of performance opportunities throughout the year from large scale main house and outdoor productions to intimate studio and dynamic street theatre performances.

Other productions written for PYT by Matt Beames include:

The Gingerbread Man (2017)

Hide (2017)

The 12 Days of Christmas (2016)

Alice's Adventures (2016)

Beauty and the Beast (2015)

www.thepointeastleigh.co.uk

Finding Truth in Fantasy

It is the responsibility of the director to open metaphorical doors for actors to walk through, to engage them in a dialogue of discovery that allows them the opportunity to make choices based on their own life experience to either sympathise or empathise with their characters. This can often be hard when playing within a fantasy setting; how do you find the truth in Stone Trolls, magic Guardians, and mystical beings? How do you sympathise with a character who uses magic to turn children into animals?

Yes, *Sleeping Beauty* is a story of Trolls and Guardians, of Dragons and Magic, but it is also a story of friendship, of working together to overcome adversity, of undertaking an act of true devotion to save someone you love. These very human traits underpin everything in this tale; that mixed with *Sleeping Beauty's* magical setting and fantastical characters make for a rip-roaring adventure perfect for children and adults alike. It has been both a challenge and a joy to bring this story to life and in doing so we discovered a beautiful piece of storytelling full of love, hope and warmth.

Matt has created a beautifully balanced script full of fantastical wonder that manages to stay rooted in human emotion, making it a treat for any cast to bring to life. When you approach this tale as a director, let yourself disappear into the adventure, fall in love with the characters and then get it on its feet; it's a story that truly does grow in the telling and I promise you will have a wonderful time doing so.

As a company, much like the tale we told, we approached the making of *Sleeping Beauty* with truth and friendship at its core, and if you do the same you're sure to fall in love with it as much as we did.

Daniel Hill

Director

November 2017

Cast

The original production was performed at The Point Theatre from the 19th to the 24th December 2017 with the following cast:

January, Middling of Winter	Katie-Anna McConnell
February, Eldest of Winter	Lucy Parkinson
March, Youngest of Spring	Kelly Lobban
April, Middling of Spring	Niall Reeves
May, Eldest of Spring	Lauren Birch
June, Youngest of Summer	Evie Tinner
July, Middling of Summer	Rosie Cunliffe
August, Eldest of Summer	Emily Pauley
September, Youngest of Autumn	Grace Taylor
October, Middling of Autumn	Rose Smith
November, Eldest of Autumn	Ben Sutcliffe
December, Youngest of Winter	Hannah-May Coull
Oublier, The Lost One	Meg Beeson
Aurora	Ellie Morrison
Dregil, a Wolf	Leah Reeves
Unferth Stoneheart, a Troll	Eoghan Butler
Gudrun, one of the Nornir	Alice White
King Peter / The Old Man	Aidan Cooper
Queen Melisende / The Old Woman	Sophie Parker
Prince Roland	Max Baker
Hunter	Klaudia Pacharew
The White Doe / Grace	Lara Clements
The Blackbird / Cole	Alexander Holt
Captain Devoir / The Iron Troll	Rhys Tabor
Young Aurora	Roma Fordham

Young Roland	Charlie Rosser
Farmer	Matt Downer
Spike, one of Oublier's servants	Holly Briard
Spine, one of Oublier's servants	Joshua Stevenson
Spur, one of Oublier's servants	Jacob Beeson
Briar, one of Oublier's servants	Joe Field
Barb, one of Oublier's servants	Molly Smith

Puppeteers

Kayleigh Benham, Grace Keeping, India Morrison

Villagers / Myrkwood Spirits

Reena Bains, Nate Barker, Daisy Blatch, Isabel Buchanan, Neve Campbell-Williams, Lara Clements, Matt Downer, Roma Fordham, Zoe Fordham, Katie George, Kayleigh Henderson, Caitlin Hooper, Maggie Jones, Tom Mepham, Tamara Meyer, Klaudia Pacharew, Macie Partridge, Charlie Rosser, Ruth Rudman, Esme Thompsett, Katie Trimmer, Eimile Woodward

Creative Team

Script by Matt Beames
Lyrics by Daniel Hill
Music by David Lewington

The creative team for the original production was:

Director	Daniel Hill
Designer	Carl Davies
Composer	David Lewington
Lighting Designer	Tim Slater
Assistant Director	India Morrison
Design Assistant	Millie Else
Stage Managers	Lily Coull
	James Henderson
Deputy Stage Manager	Lewis Mullins
Assistant Stage Managers	Joshua Brierley
	Holly Scott
Technicians	Shaun Hobbs
	Ashton Partridge
Head Chaperone	Trudie Cooper

Introduction

I've always believed that stories are important, that they live and grow in us when we hear them and when we tell them, and for me this adaptation of Sleeping Beauty is no exception. In exploring the early versions of the story I came across a theory that the tale was an indication of the shift from a thirteen month lunar year to a solar year, with twelve fairies invited to the naming feast and one forgotten. Almost immediately I saw twelve months, guardians of the year, who keep the world turning in the best way possible – by telling stories...

I buried myself in the original French tale, Germanic folklore and Norse mythology, and a story began to form. It was a tale of a kingdom overrun by an enchanted forest, and a young woman on a journey to try and save her childhood friend. As I began to write I fell in love with the world and the characters in it.

The princess of the original versions plays quite a passive role so it was a delight to turn this on its head, giving Aurora the heroic quest to save her friend, with courageous companions to help her on the way. From the outset this was a story about friendship rather than romance. Aurora's quest is driven by a desire to help her friend and friendship drives Dregil, Gudrun and Unferth to join her. I believe the bonds of friendship can be strongest of all.

The importance of friendship in this story has also been inspired by the amazing young people and creative team of The Point Youth Theatre. Their passion for telling this story and bringing Aurora's world to life, and the strength of their bond as a company is incredibly inspiring, and I am extremely proud that my first published script is a show written for this tremendous group.

Matt Beames

November 2017

SLEEPING BEAUTY

Characters

January, Middling of Winter
February, Eldest of Winter
March, Youngest of Spring
April, Middling of Spring
May, Eldest of Spring
June, Youngest of Summer
July, Middling of Summer
August, Eldest of Summer
September, Youngest of Autumn
October, Middling of Autumn
November, Eldest of Autumn
December, Youngest of Winter
Oublier, The Lost One

Aurora
Dregil, a Wolf
Unferth Stoneheart, a Troll
Gudrun, one of the Nornir

King Peter/The Old Man
Queen Melisende/The Old Woman
Prince Roland
Hunter
The White Doe/Grace
The Blackbird/Cole

Captain Devoir/The Iron Troll
Young Aurora
Young Roland
Farmer
Villagers

Spike, one of Oublier's servants
Spine, one of Oublier's servants
Spur, one of Oublier's servants
Briar, one of Oublier's servants
Barb, one of Oublier's servants

Myrkwood Spirits

Note

Most characters are written to be as gender fluid as possible. If in some dialogue a gender is referred to that doesn't match the performer's gender, it can be changed.

ACT ONE

We are in a place that is both real and unreal. This is where the twelve months, the Guardians of the Year gather each month to tell stories, and so move the world forward in its cycle. There is a fire in the middle of the stage, and about it are thirteen different seats. Each one is different, ideally suited to the month who always uses it. One seat, the thirteenth, is dusty and long unused. The twelve Guardians enter, some alone, some in pairs or small groups.

År Etter År (Year After Year)

GUARDIANS   År etter år
Etter år
Etter år

Come one, come all, to the gathering of time
Where magic drifts along a fine mystic line
Where memories arrive like a long lost friend
Where journey's start meets journey's end

Year after year, we start anew
As time moves on, it moves with you
As memories slowly drift back into sight
It's hope that wins the yearly fight

Come one, come all, to the gathering of time
Where magic drifts along a fine mystic line
Where memories arrive like a long lost friend
Where journey's start meets journey's end

They sit in their respective seats (progressing round the circle anti-clockwise), facing the centre. It feels informal, a gathering of companions. The empty seat is to December's right.

JULY   Here we are again.

SEPTEMBER Circles and cycles, July, every single time!

MARCH Can't you think of something else to say?

FEBRUARY Hush now, young ones. Consider the occasion.

JUNE This is hardly the first December...

AUGUST Not for you, perhaps...

MAY True enough.

A moment. The other Guardians all turn their attention to December, who is a little shy and awkward.

NOVEMBER Welcome, Sister.

DECEMBER Hi.

JANUARY Almost a year it has been since you took up December's mantle.

OCTOBER You have watched with us as the months pass.

APRIL As the seasons change.

NOVEMBER And now Autumn has ended.

DECEMBER And Winter must begin.

MAY Your first Winter.

AUGUST Your first December.

NOVEMBER Your first story.

FEBRUARY Are you ready?

DECEMBER I think so.

December looks about the circle, uncertain.

JANUARY Relax, Sister.

MARCH You'll be fine.

SEPTEMBER She was always nervous, too.

DECEMBER   She?

NOVEMBER   Your predecessor.

JANUARY   The last December.

FEBRUARY   But you know that, don't you?

DECEMBER   Yes... I remember her, a little... I am her, as well as myself. It's strange.

MAY   That is to be expected. December was the first of us to... die...

JULY   But you took up her mantle.

AUGUST   Twelve Guardians there are.

MAY   Twelve there must be.

NOVEMBER   Twelve there have always been.

DECEMBER   But... Whose is the thirteenth seat?

Silence.

DECEMBER   I've wanted to ask for so long...

FEBRUARY   That is a dark story.

MARCH   The story of the Lost One.

OCTOBER   A tale of a world where beauty slept, and sorrow reigned.

DECEMBER   I remember parts of it, but not all.

JANUARY   Perhaps that is best.

JUNE   But surely–

SEPTEMBER   Hush now. December must choose the story she will tell.

DECEMBER   It's my choice?

MAY   Yours alone.

NOVEMBER   Your tale will move the seasons onward, out of Autumn and into Winter.

DECEMBER   Then... I will tell the tale of A World Where Beauty Sleeps.

FEBRUARY   No!

MARCH   Why not?

JULY   It's her choice, after all.

AUGUST   But it is about December's ending.

APRIL   But also about her beginning.

MARCH   I will help you tell it, Sister.

SEPTEMBER   As will I.

JUNE   And I.

OCTOBER   I too.

MAY   Each as foolish as the next!

NOVEMBER   To tell a tale is to live it, young one. You must understand that.

DECEMBER   I do.

NOVEMBER   Very well. Your choice is made. We will honour it.

FEBRUARY   This is a bad idea.

JANUARY   She has chosen her story. Now we must help her to tell it.

NOVEMBER   Then let us begin.

The Guardians all stand, becoming formal; this is a ritual. They each speak, and as they have spoken sit once more.

JANUARY   I am January, and I have told my tale.

FEBRUARY   I am February, and I have told my tale.

MARCH I am March, and I have told my tale.

APRIL I am April, and I have told my tale.

MAY I am May, and I have told my tale.

JUNE I am June, and I have told my tale.

JULY I am July, and I have told my tale.

AUGUST I am August, and I have told my tale.

SEPTEMBER I am September, and I have told my tale.

OCTOBER I am October, and I have told my tale.

NOVEMBER I am November, and I have told my tale.

DECEMBER I am December, and this shall be my tale.

The fire fades and the space changes, becoming the world of the story. December begins to tell the tale, joined by the other Guardians.

DECEMBER So it begins. The setting is a prosperous kingdom, a land of peace and plenty.

The kingdom comes to life. We see the people of this land working together in the fields. People are cheerful, good tempered, working together for the benefit of all.

Golden Sun (Working Song)

VILLAGERS Golden sun sets on a Summer's night
Glistening dew on an Autumn morn
Glowing fires on a Winters eve
Gleeful babes on a fresh Spring day

OCTOBER As the world spins and the years pass, the people work hard and reap the rewards.

JUNE But peace and prosperity do not always last, and even the brightest days have their shadows...

A crack of thunder, perhaps flashes of lightning. All stop and look towards it. A sound, perhaps of thorns ripping through the earth... the curse has fallen.

DECEMBER   As this tale opens, it is a time where the beauty and balance of the world lies sleeping, and strangeness and sorrow reign.

The kingdom in turmoil, fear is rampant. Shadows grow at the edges of the space, perhaps the people huddle together during the following.

FEBRUARY   The architect of this sorrow is Oublier, the Lost One...

MAY   In the castle at the centre of this land Prince Roland,

JUNE   heir to the throne and beloved of the people,

MAY   lies in an enchanted sleep.

AUGUST   About the castle a forest of thorns has grown.

JANUARY   Spreading outward with every passing day.

NOVEMBER   The King and Queen are missing.

APRIL   And the people of the land have no one to guide them in their sorrows...

The people of the kingdom are afraid, ready to flee their homes. A Farmer enters, returning from the fields and struggling against the tide of people.

FARMER   What's happening?

VILLAGER   We're leaving. All of us.

VILLAGER   Not everyone.

VILLAGER   Anyone with sense.

FARMER   Why?

VILLAGER　　Why do you think!?

VILLAGER　　The Myrkwood's growing, it's not safe.

VILLAGER　　The Prince is cursed to sleep, the King and Queen missing...

VILLAGER　　We're getting out while we can.

Alfons Devoir, the Captain of the Castle Guard comes with soldiers, trying to keep order.

DEVOIR　　Keep moving if you're going, this is a public road, not a picnic spot!

FARMER　　Captain Devoir?

DEVOIR　　What's the trouble here?

VILLAGER　　No trouble Captain, just giving some advice.

FARMER　　I'll not leave my home!

VILLAGER　　On your head be it, old fool!

DEVOIR　　Come on, you need to clear the road! If you're going I wish you luck.

VILLAGER　　And to you Captain.

The villagers move on, and Devoir stands with the Farmer.

FARMER　　Is it as bad as they say, Captain?

DEVOIR　　Worse my friend, if truth be told. The curse Oublier laid on the Prince has fallen, and the Myrkwood is overrunning everything in the land.

FARMER　　They said as much.

DEVOIR　　But the forest... changes. The paths seem to shift so that you lose your way... and there are... things... Strange things in the darkness, and the Lost One herself has been seen haunting the shadows... Maybe they're right to flee...

FARMER   But this is home! I can't abandon it.

DEVOIR   I know how you feel. I was born here, my duty is here. I'm staying.

FARMER   What will happen to us? What can we do?

DEVOIR   I don't know, old one. Take each day as it comes.

FARMER   And hope.

DEVOIR   As long as we can. I must go, I'm heading for the castle.

FARMER   But it's overrun!

DEVOIR   Aye. But I have my duty, and I'll not set it aside.

FARMER   Good luck, Captain.

DEVOIR   And to you.

Lost in Shadow

VILLAGERS   Golden sun sets on a Summer's night
Glistening dew on an Autumn morn
Glowing fires on a Winter's eve
Gleeful babes on a fresh Spring day

These are the things that nature provides
Golden, Glistening, Glowing, Glee
But now that nature has turned the tide
We run in darkness, in fear we hide

GUARDIANS   Golden sunsets lost in shadow
Glistening dew lost to rain
Glowing fires lost to cold
Gleeful babes lost in time

The days have changed
The nights grow long

Daylight's kiss can't beat the storm
We watch, we wait
We hope, we pray
That shadow's touch won't rule the day

Lost in shadow

Devoir and the Farmer move off, and the crowds of people filter off too, leaving the Guardians alone.

FEBRUARY   And so the shadows have grown and the Myrkwood spreads further each day,

APRIL   an impenetrable labyrinth filled with shadows and spirits.

MARCH   Oublier herself moves among the thorns,

JULY   plaguing those who cling to their homes,

OCTOBER   refusing to flee.

DECEMBER   The world turns and the cycle of seasons pass,

SEPTEMBER and as Winter begins a young woman enters the shadowed forest of thorns,

JANUARY   bringing with her curious companions...

Aurora, Unferth, Gudrun and Dregil enter. They look about them, curious. Perhaps the Guardians hide themselves at the edges of the space to watch.

UNFERTH   Are we there yet?

GUDRUN   One hundred and thirty-six.

UNFERTH   What?

GUDRUN   You've asked that question one hundred and thirty-six times since lunchtime.

SEPTEMBER Remind you of anyone, March?

FEBRUARY   Hush!

UNFERTH   Well, y'know, I'm just wondering is all.

GUDRUN   Do you see a castle?

Unferth looks carefully about. Dregil moves about the space, sniffing, investigating.

UNFERTH   Erm... No.

GUDRUN   Then we can't be there yet, can we?

UNFERTH   I don't know, do I? This is Aurora's homeland, not mine!

AURORA   Calm down you two. No, Unferth, we're not there yet. Not at the castle, anyway. But I think this must be the start of the Myrkwood.

Dregil moves to stand by Aurora's side.

DREGIL   You are right. This is not a natural forest; doesn't smell right.

UNFERTH   Can't tell the difference myself...

GUDRUN   Now there's a surprise.

UNFERTH   What's that mean?

GUDRUN   Well, Mountain Trolls are hardly famed for their sense of smell, are they?

UNFERTH   And I suppose you Nornir are, eh?

GUDRUN   I don't need smell to tell this isn't a natural forest. Feels wrong.

AURORA   I feel it too.

Dregil nudges her hand and sits.

DREGIL   We should rest here tonight. Wait till morning to head in further.

AURORA   Sensible plan, I think.

GUDRUN   I agree.

The four make a quick camp and settle themselves for the night.

UNFERTH   How does it feel to be home, Aurora?

AURORA   It's strange. It's not...

GUDRUN   Not what you were expecting?

AURORA   No.

UNFERTH   Well, scary sorceress cursing your boyfriend and the entire kingdom will do that, I suppose.

Gudrun hits Unferth.

UNFERTH   What?

AURORA   I keep telling you, he's not my boyfriend!

UNFERTH   Well if you say so, but it seems a lot of effort for someone you hardly know...

GUDRUN   I think we should probably get some sleep, don't you?

DREGIL   Unferth will take first watch.

UNFERTH   Me?

GUDRUN   Yes!

They settle to sleep, Unferth perhaps muttering to himself as he watches. The others fall asleep, and perhaps Unferth begins to doze... The Guardians move out of their hiding places and begin to investigate.

DECEMBER   Who are they?

FEBRUARY   Strangers. Except this one. She has a trace of this land on her...

MARCH   They said she had come home...

SEPTEMBER   But where from?

JUNE   And where did she get such strange companions?

One of the Guardians moves too close to Unferth and he wakes.

UNFERTH   Eh? Who are you lot?

NOVEMBER   Please don't be alarmed.

Dregil wakes and leaps to defend Aurora.

DREGIL   Aurora!

UNFERTH   Gudrun, we've got company!

Aurora and Gudrun wake and prepare for a fight.

DECEMBER   Please, wait!

MAY   Be calm, everyone!

APRIL   We mean no harm!

UNFERTH   So you say, you bunch of bugs!

FEBRUARY   Bugs?

JULY   How dare you!

AURORA   Enough!

Everyone stops.

AURORA   Unferth, they're not bugs, obviously. Now, what say we begin again?

NOVEMBER   Excellent idea, young lady.

AURORA   I am Aurora, and these are my friends. Gudrun, Unferth, and this is Dregil. You startled us.

DECEMBER   I'm sorry. We are the Months of the Year.

GUDRUN   The Guardians?

UNFERTH   You know this lot?

GUDRUN   I've heard of them. It is an honour to meet you.

FEBRUARY   Thank you, my dear.

MAY   We apologise for disturbing your rest...

SEPTEMBER   But we were curious about you.

AURORA   We're just travellers.

JULY   Ah, but you're not exactly a typical set of companions, are you?

GUDRUN   Perhaps not.

FEBRUARY   What brings you to this land, young lady?

UNFERTH   We might ask what you lot are doing here as well.

DREGIL   Friend Unferth is not polite, but he does have a point.

GUDRUN   I understood that the Twelve Guardians stood over the whole world, watching and guiding the seasons in their passing...

MARCH   And so we do.

AURORA   Then what brings you, all of you, here?

FEBRUARY   There is a curse laid upon this land, as you must already know.

DECEMBER   Prince Roland, heir to the throne, lies sleeping in the castle at the centre of the Myrkwood.

MAY   And this enchanted forest grows day by day.

JUNE   We cannot act against it, not directly, but we can watch, and...

OCTOBER   Offer guidance.

AURORA   But why?

NOVEMBER Because...

DECEMBER It's partly our fault.

FEBRUARY December!

DECEMBER But—

MAY   You speak out of turn!

DECEMBER I'm only telling the truth!

A strange light and noise fills the space and it slowly changes to a banquet hall. Aurora and her companions are confused.

AURORA   What's happening?

MARCH   Prince Roland is dreaming.

UNFERTH   What?

FEBRUARY   This forest, the Prince's slumber, they're part of the same curse.

NOVEMBER   When Prince Roland dreams, sometimes they become a part of the forest...

AURORA   This is a dream?

GUDRUN   Looks more like a banquet hall...

UNFERTH   Ooh, is there any food?

JULY   Not real food, I'm afraid...

The vision has fully manifested now. We are in the great hall of the castle, and it is 17 years in the past.

SEPTEMBER I remember this!

AUGUST   Prince Roland's Naming Day Feast.

AURORA   Roland...

UNFERTH   How can you remember it?

APRIL   We were invited.

DECEMBER   This was the beginning.

AURORA   The beginning of what?

FEBRUARY   Better take our places...

The Guardians become part of the vision, taking their places in the banquet hall.

UNFERTH   What do we do?

GUDRUN   It doesn't look like they can see us...

AURORA   Guess we watch and see what happens then...

Aurora and her companions find a place to watch the proceedings. The King and Queen enter. The Queen carries baby Roland.

KING   Friends, honoured guests, thank you for joining us on this special day.

QUEEN   It is our son's Naming Day.

KING   To all of you gathered here, we present Prince Roland!

ALL   Prince Roland!

Devoir leads a cheer for Prince Roland, and all join in. The Queen places the baby in a cot at the centre of the space. The baby begins to cry.

UNFERTH   Bit of a whinger, isn't he?

GUDRUN   Hush!

KING   Thank you all for your gifts and good wishes, and for being here with us on this special day.

QUEEN   We'd especially like to thank our honoured guests for joining us. Guardians of the Year... You are most welcome.

FEBRUARY Our thanks to you, Queen Melisende, King
   Peter.

MAY You do us great honour by asking us here.

AUGUST We are glad to welcome the young Prince to
his naming, and we beg leave to bestow our blessings on
him.

QUEEN But, you are the Guardians of the Year!

KING We would not dare ask such a gift of you!

NOVEMBER But we would offer them, good King.

QUEEN Then we gratefully accept.

*The Guardians step forward, gathering in a circle about the
cot. This has the feeling of a ritual.*

JANUARY The world spins.

FEBRUARY The cycle of seasons turns.

MARCH The years pass one after the other.

APRIL And with each passing year

MAY You will grow stronger

JUNE Braver

JULY More beloved.

AUGUST Young heart

SEPTEMBER Future King

OCTOBER Grow well

NOVEMBER Live well

*As December is about to speak, perhaps a flash of light and
a crack of thunder, and all onstage react. Oublier enters,
angry, dark and forbidding.*

OUBLIER I'm sorry, did I interrupt?

AUGUST   You!

OUBLIER   Yes, brothers and sisters. Me.

KING   Guardians... Who is this?

OUBLIER   This, little King, is one who was once as grand as these twelve you seem so keen to worship.

QUEEN   I don't understand...

MAY   This is our one-time sister.

DECEMBER   She was once part of our Order.

OUBLIER   Yes, but no longer, eh little Sister?

DECEMBER   Mercy...

OUBLIER   Don't call me that! They took our names, remember? They gave each of you a new one, but I... I was forgotten. So I took one for myself.

FEBRUARY   What name, Sister?

OUBLIER   I am Oublier.

QUEEN   My Lady Oublier, why have you come here?

OUBLIER   Why, I heard that there was a little one to be named of course! I heard whispers of a great feast, of celebration, gifts to be given, with the Twelve Guardians of the Year as guests of honour!

OCTOBER   Sister, what do you want?

OUBLIER   I simply wondered why I had not been invited?

QUEEN   Good lady, we did not know–

OUBLIER   And you shall suffer for it!

AUGUST   Enough! Your quarrel is not with them!

OUBLIER   But it is, of course it is! With them and all the others! I had a place, a purpose! And then they, these stupid, short-lived nothings, changed it.

MAY   We serve the world and the people in it. However they need us to.

OUBLIER   Which is all well and good, May, until they decide they no longer need you! You are the Twelve Guardians of the Year. But once you were Thirteen!

JULY   Times change, Sister.

OUBLIER   Times and calendars and the memories of humans, perhaps. Not everything.

AURORA   Calendars?

DECEMBER   I think you should leave.

OUBLIER   Not yet. Not until I have bestowed my... gift... on the little Prince.

KING   Your gift, my Lady?

OUBLIER   Yes!

APRIL   We cannot let you, Sister.

OUBLIER   You cannot stop me!

Oublier moves to the cot, casting those who would stop her aside. She lays the curse upon Prince Roland.

Døden Være Over Deg (Death be Upon You)

OUBLIER   Døden være over deg
Death be upon you

Before the day the babe becomes a boy
Upon his sixteenth birthday
He'll touch his finger that bears a ring
Upon a sharpened spindle

That day will be his last on earth
As he draws his final breath
And darkness takes away the light
So all he'll know is death

Death be upon you

Oublier exits, and the King and Queen rush to their child.

KING   My son...

QUEEN   What will happen to you?

JANUARY   We cannot undo it.

KING   But you watch over us, you're so powerful!

JUNE   Oublier was once one of our Order. We cannot undo what she has done.

DECEMBER   Maybe I can...

AUGUST   December?

MARCH   What are you talking about?

DECEMBER   I never laid my blessing on the Prince.

NOVEMBER   It's true, she was interrupted.

MAY   But you cannot break the curse!

DECEMBER   But maybe I can... turn it aside a little.

QUEEN   My Lady December, we have no right to ask, but...

DECEMBER   But I may offer.

Sove Være Over Deg (Sleep be Upon You)

DECEMBER   Sove Være Over Deg
  Sleep be upon you

Before the day the babe becomes a boy
Upon his sixteenth birthday
He'll touch his finger that bears a ring
Upon a sharpened spindle

That day won't be his last on earth
As sleep becomes his only notion
He'll lie at peace until the day
He's woken by an act of true devotion

Sleep be upon you

As the blessing finishes the dream vision fades. The banquet hall becomes the forest once more, with only the Guardians and Aurora and her companions present.

AURORA   Well, that was...

GUDRUN   Enlightening.

UNFERTH   Downright odd is what that was.

AURORA   You said Roland was dreaming?

FEBRUARY   Yes.

GUDRUN   But what we just saw, that happened.

APRIL   It did.

AURORA   So was it a dream or a memory?

FEBRUARY   Yes.

AURORA   That's not an answer...

APRIL   I'm afraid not, no.

UNFERTH   I'm not sure I like you lot very much.

AURORA   Does it happen often?

AUGUST   It's hard to say, the Myrkwood is so vast now... It's very possible that there are visions manifesting constantly, in different parts of the forest.

DECEMBER It's another part of Oublier's revenge, you see.

AURORA But why is she doing this?

UNFERTH It seemed to me that she had a bone to pick with you lot more than anyone else.

DREGIL A little more respect, perhaps, my friend.

UNFERTH What do you mean? I'm just saying what I see, that's all!

GUDRUN I have heard stories from times past that our year was split into thirteen parts, not twelve...

AURORA Is that true?

A moment as the Guardians consider.

NOVEMBER Aye, it's true enough. Once men followed the silver moon's path, breaking the year into thirteen parts.

APRIL But times change.

SEPTEMBER Mankind chose to follow the sun instead.

MAY And that gave twelve months to a year.

JUNE We each took a new name, but our sister...

MARCH She was lost.

DECEMBER Forgotten.

GUDRUN Until she chose to seek revenge...

AURORA But why Roland? He didn't do anything!

AUGUST We don't know.

AURORA Why didn't you stop it?

FEBRUARY We cannot interfere.

AURORA But you are the Twelve Guardians!

NOVEMBER   Of the year, Aurora.

AUGUST   We ensure the world spins and the seasons change.

JANUARY   We cannot interfere in the lives of men or beasts.

DECEMBER   Even when we might wish to.

Pause.

GUDRUN   What did the King and Queen do?

APRIL   It was decreed that none in the lands near the castle would own spindle or wheel to make thread.

SEPTEMBER   All cloth was made on outlying farms.

MARCH   They hoped their precautions would be enough.

Pause. The night has passed, and morning is lightening the sky.

UNFERTH   Dawn's coming, Aurora.

AURORA   Time we were moving on then.

JULY   Where will you go, young lady?

AURORA   Further into the forest.

MARCH   What for?

AURORA   To find the castle.

JUNE   Why?

UNFERTH   Why do you think?

FEBRUARY   You think you four can lift the curse?

DREGIL   Not we four.

UNFERTH   Just my lady Aurora.

AURORA   I don't know if I can, but... I have a duty.

DECEMBER   But so many others have been lost in the attempt!

AURORA   I have to try. He's my friend.

NOVEMBER   You have a courageous heart, Aurora.

APRIL   And most curious companions... How did you come by them?

UNFERTH   What does that mean?

AURORA   They're my friends.

GUDRUN   When Aurora spoke of her intentions, we chose to journey with her.

DREGIL   We go where she goes because that's where we choose to be.

AURORA   You truly cannot aid us?

AUGUST   We cannot. But we watch over the forest as best we can, and we may yet see you again.

AURORA   Then we bid you farewell for now.

DECEMBER   Farewell Aurora.

The Guardians move off, though perhaps some remain in the shadows, watching. Aurora and her companions break camp and begin to journey onward.

UNFERTH   They were an odd lot.

GUDRUN   They are the Guardians. They stand above all of us, over everything.

UNFERTH   They didn't do much standing as far as I can see, more hovering.

GUDRUN   You're hopeless!

AURORA   I thought they were nice enough.

Dregil nudges her hand.

DREGIL   But they still left us to find our own way.

AURORA   Well, I didn't know they'd be here, so it's not like I was aiming on asking their help.

GUDRUN   True enough.

UNFERTH   I don't like these woods very much. Creepy.

GUDRUN   I thought trolls were supposed to like nature.

UNFERTH   Not all trolls are the same, you know. Forest Trolls love a forest, as you might expect. Hill Trolls too, to an extent. Us Mountain Trolls though… We're much more about wide skies and grey stone. And anyway, there's not a lot about this place that's natural, if you ask me.

AURORA   It's so quiet…

UNFERTH   Exactly! We've seen no wildlife at all since we arrived. It's not normal.

There is a whistle of birdsong, and the companions freeze for a moment, listening. The Blackbird appears, perhaps coming to land on Unferth.

GUDRUN   Famous last words, eh Unferth.

UNFERTH   Shoo!

Unferth shoos the Blackbird, and it flutters away clearly offended. Perhaps Dregil moves closer to it, sniffing…

AURORA   It doesn't seem very frightened.

Suddenly Dregil is alert, looking off. The others notice.

UNFERTH   Still, one blackbird hardly makes up for…

DREGIL   Hush!

As they watch, hands perhaps on weapons, the White Doe enters, moving warily.

AURORA   She's beautiful…

The Blackbird flies over to the White Doe and lands on her back. As the companions watch, the White Doe and the Blackbird exit.

GUDRUN   I've never seen anything like that.

AURORA   No. It was like they were friends...

UNFERTH   More and more odd, this place.

AURORA   But why did they run?

DREGIL   Someone is coming.

Again the party ready themselves, and after a moment a Hunter enters, armed with a bow and clearly stalking something. The Hunter notices Aurora and Gudrun, and straightens.

HUNTER   Greetings strangers. I had not thought to meet–

Hunter notices Dregil.

HUNTER   Look out, wolf!

As Hunter aims at Dregil, the wolf readies himself, growling. Aurora leaps in front of him, shielding him.

AURORA   Wait! He will not hurt you!

UNFERTH   Unless you try and shoot him. Then he'll probably crunch your face off...

HUNTER   A troll?

UNFERTH   Oh, look out, we've got a clever one here...

GUDRUN   Peace, Unferth.

AURORA   Please, don't be afraid. We mean you no harm. I am Aurora, and these are my companions. This is Gudrun, Unferth, and this is Dregil.

HUNTER   I am sorry. I had not thought to meet such a curious party, and… this forest is full of tricks. I am called Hunter.

UNFERTH   Can't imagine why…

GUDRUN   Shut up, you stone lummox. Pleased to meet you Hunter. What were you stalking?

HUNTER   I am seeking a white doe, which wanders this forest accompanied by a blackbird. Have you seen them?

AURORA   They're a strange pair, there's something beautiful about them.

HUNTER   When did you see them?

GUDRUN   They passed through just before you got here.

HUNTER   Please, which way did they go?

Gudrun gestures, and Dregil looks to Unferth.

DREGIL   What do you want with them?

HUNTER   I have to cut out their hearts.

Dregil growls ominously.

AURORA   Why?

GUDRUN   Surely not for food? The doe was young, and the bird younger.

HUNTER   I have no choice. I have to do it.

Hunter makes as though to exit, but Dregil leaps to block him. Unferth moves to stand beside the wolf.

UNFERTH   You're not going anywhere till you explain yourself.

HUNTER   Please, you must let me pass!

DREGIL   Talk first.

Hunter tries to pass, but Unferth and Dregil block him. Finally in frustration Hunter cries out.

HUNTER   She took my brother and sister!

Pause. Hunter slumps, defeated. Aurora moves toward him, curious.

AURORA   Who took them?

HUNTER   The Lost One.

GUDRUN   Oublier?

HUNTER   We live not far from here, in the house our parents built. They're gone now, lost to fever five years back. We stayed, working the land together. Then the Prince's curse fell and the Myrkwood began to spread... But we carried on, and we get by. I hunt, my brother and sister grow a few crops.

AURORA   What are they like?

HUNTER   My sister Grace is beautiful. Her skin is pale as moonlight, and she is the gentlest girl in the world. My brother Cole... He is excitable, always flitting from one job to the next, whistling all the while...

AURORA   What happened to them?

HUNTER   One evening as we were sitting down to eat there was a knock at the door. Unusual enough, even before the Myrkwood came... It was Oublier, the Lost One herself.

GUDRUN   What did she want?

HUNTER   She told us we had to go. She taunted us, threatened us, swore her dark servants would plague us every day till we fled.

UNFERTH   What did you do?

HUNTER   We refused. Our parents built that house, and we'd made it our own with hard work. We'd lost them; we wouldn't lose our home.

UNFERTH   Brave of you.

HUNTER   Or foolish, perhaps. Oublier laughed at us then, and it made me furious... I told her to leave or I'd throw her out. Then she got angry, and... It must have been a spell, for there was a flash of light and then I remembered nothing for a long while. When I opened my eyes I was lying on the floor, and I was alone.

AURORA   Your brother and sister?

HUNTER   I searched and searched, but Cole and Grace were nowhere to be found. Finally I came back to the house that evening, and Oublier was waiting for me.

Oublier has entered, conjured by Hunter's telling. This is not a dream vision, just Hunter's memory.

OUBLIER   It doesn't pay to defy me, child. If you wish to see your siblings again, you must search through the Myrkwood for the White Doe and the Blackbird that wander together. Find them, hunt them, and if you cut out their hearts, you will be reunited with your brother and sister.

Oublier disappears. The White Doe and Blackbird enter again, unseen by all except Dregil; the others are focused on Hunter.

AURORA   I'm sorry.

GUDRUN   What did you do?

HUNTER   What could I do? I took up my bow and set out into the Myrkwood. I have found traces of the two creatures, even seen them, but they keep eluding me.

AURORA   But how do you know Oublier was speaking the truth?

GUDRUN   She is a treacherous, vile thing.

Dregil moves toward the Doe, which is wary but does not run. He moves close till they are perhaps nose to nose, and they are clearly talking to each other.

HUNTER   What choice do I have? I couldn't find Cole and Grace, and they wouldn't have left our home. All I can do is try and find the doe and the blackbird, and do as the Lost One has said. But I can never get close...

Unferth has noticed Dregil now.

UNFERTH   Oh, I don't know about that...

The others look, and Hunter scrambles to nock an arrow to his bow. Perhaps the Blackbird whistles, and Dregil turns, looking at Unferth.

DREGIL   They are not as they seem...

AURORA   Wait, Hunter.

HUNTER   I have to.

Hunter draws and aims at the Blackbird, and Dregil charges toward him.

AURORA   No!

Dregil leaps, knocking Hunter backward as he looses the arrow. The arrow clips the Blackbird's wing and it tumbles to the ground. Aurora rushes to it, as does the White Doe. Dregil is on top of Hunter, preventing him moving.

HUNTER   Let me go!

GUDRUN   Calm yourself, Hunter.

UNFERTH   Dregil's just saved your brother's life.

HUNTER   What?

DREGIL   Your siblings have been enchanted, changed into animal shape.

AURORA   Oublier is wicked and cruel. Hunter, the White Doe and Blackbird are Grace and Cole.

UNFERTH   If you'd killed them, they'd have changed back right enough.

Dregil moves off Hunter, who rises as the White Doe moves towards him.

HUNTER   Sister?

The Doe nods, and nuzzles his hand.

HUNTER   What have I done?

Aurora gently sets the Blackbird on the ground, and it hops over to Hunter.

AURORA   He's okay. You clipped his wing, but he'll be fine.

HUNTER   I'm so sorry.

AURORA   Look, no real harm done.

HUNTER   But what can I do? How can I change them back?

Aurora and her companions think. Unseen, December approaches alone, watching them.

GUDRUN   Names... There is something in true names, there must be...

HUNTER   What are you talking about?

DREGIL   Be easy, Hunter.

AURORA   Gudrun is one of the Nornir. She sees the threads of lives as they are woven.

DECEMBER   And she sees well.

As she speaks December moves forward, becoming visible to Aurora and her companions. The group react to her appearance.

AURORA   You?

UNFERTH   What about the rest of them?

DECEMBER   Oh, it's just me.

UNFERTH   What do you want?

DECEMBER   To help.

DREGIL   What about your rules?

December hesitates, conflicted.

DECEMBER   I...

Aurora approaches December, speaks gently.

AURORA   You said Gudrun sees well. What did you mean?

DECEMBER   Your thinking is right, Gudrun. There is great power in names, and in true names especially.

A moment as Gudrun considers this.

UNFERTH   Well I don't think that's very helpful...

DECEMBER   I'm sorry, I can't...

AURORA   It's okay.

GUDRUN   True names... Okay. What if...?

UNFERTH   I can hear your brain going round, you know...

DREGIL   Unferth!

GUDRUN   Everyone, hush! Hunter, place your hand on her head. Close your eyes and think of your sister. Hold her image in your mind, and speak her true name, the one you hold in your heart.

Hunter does as Gudrun bids.

HUNTER   Grace Orphelin.

A shimmering of magic, and the enchantment on the White Doe is lifted. She is transformed into Hunter's sister, Grace.

GRACE   Hunter?

They embrace. Gudrun turns to December, perhaps bows.

GUDRUN   Thank you.

HUNTER   Now then, little brother.

Hunter crouches and the Blackbird hops onto his hand.

HUNTER   Cole Orphelin.

Again a shimmering of magic, but this time something is different. The Blackbird is unchanged.

HUNTER   Why didn't it work?

GUDRUN   The arrow clipped his wing...

AURORA   But he's alright!

HUNTER   I didn't do what Oublier said!

DECEMBER   But you tried to.

GUDRUN   Just that is enough to hold the enchantment in place?

HUNTER   What else can we do?

DECEMBER   I'm sorry.

UNFERTH   We could just defeat her, of course.

AURORA   What?

UNFERTH   Well, it stands to reason, doesn't it? She put the enchantment on in the first place, but if Aurora lifts the Prince's curse and defeats what's-her-face, her other spells will be lifted too...

DECEMBER   You also see well, Stonebrother.

GUDRUN   You're full of surprises, Unferth.

UNFERTH   Charming.

DREGIL   We should move on, Aurora.

GUDRUN   Thank you for your help.

DECEMBER   Oh, I didn't do anything, really.

AURORA   Will you come along with us?

DECEMBER   I'd... better not.

AURORA   Will we see you again?

DECEMBER   You may yet, Aurora. You may.

Perhaps December moves away, becoming an unseen watcher again.

HUNTER   But what about Cole?

GRACE   What will my brother do till the Lost One is defeated?

The Blackbird trills and flutters to land on Unferth. He listens for a moment.

UNFERTH   He says he wants to come along with us.

HUNTER   What?

GRACE   You really want to go with them?

The Blackbird trills.

HUNTER   Can he, my Lady?

AURORA   Of course.

GRACE   Thank you!

HUNTER   Be careful, little brother. Thank you, my friends.

DREGIL   It is well. Guard your sister, and we will keep your brother safe.

Hunter nods solemnly.

AURORA   Journey safe, Hunter. We will get Cole
home to you as soon as we can!

*Hunter and Grace exit, and Aurora and her companions
move on. The Guardians move forward, considering Aurora
and her companions.*

NOVEMBER   December...

DECEMBER   She handled that well.

FEBRUARY   It wasn't just her though, was it?

DECEMBER   Even so, it makes you wonder...

JUNE   What?

Is She the One?

DECEMBER   Is this the time to look to the light?
Is she the one to make things right?

DECEMBER AND FEBRUARY Can their friendship end
this pain?

GUARDIANS Will their trials bring an end to the rain?

You don't have to be strong to win the fight
You don't need to be brave to do what's right
You don't need to laugh to stop yourself from crying
You can still be a hero even with a fear of dying

Is this the time we can start to see?
Is she the one who'll set us all free?
Can their friendship end this dark?
Is she our hero, our own Joan of Arc?

You don't have to be strong to win the fight
You don't need to be brave to do what's right
You don't need to laugh to stop yourself from crying
You can still be a hero even with a fear of dying
You can still be a hero even with a fear of dying

The party move along through the forest again. Cole rides on Unferth's shoulder.

UNFERTH   Don't get too comfortable, pipsqueak. If you poop on me, I'll swat you into next week!

AURORA   Do you know how far it is to the castle at the centre of the Myrkwood, Cole?

UNFERTH   He says no. But he'll try and find a way above the canopy and have a look if you like?

AURORA   No, it's alright, I just–

A strange light and noise fills the space once more; this is another dream vision. The space begins to change, becoming the courtyard of the castle. The companions gather together, prepared for anything.

AURORA   What now?

UNFERTH   It's another one of those vision-things!

AURORA   But this looks like...

UNFERTH   I don't like these things. It's not normal!

GUDRUN   We're travelling through an enchanted forest of thorns to rescue a sleeping prince from a curse. What's normal?

The space is now fully changed. We're in the courtyard of the castle, 10 years ago. A young girl is sitting in the courtyard beside a cart loaded with bundles of wool and fleece, spinning yarn using a drop spindle. Aurora clearly recognises her. She moves closer, but the girl does not see her.

GUDRUN   Looks like a castle courtyard.

UNFERTH   Must be I suppose. But when is this? And who's the girl?

AURORA   It's the castle courtyard, yes. As to when, it's ten years ago.

GUDRUN   How can you be so sure?

AURORA   Because this is me.

UNFERTH   You?

AURORA   Yes.

UNFERTH   Bit of a squirt, weren't you?

GUDRUN   Aurora, if that's you, perhaps you shouldn't get so close...

Aurora waves her hand directly in front of young Aurora. She doesn't react.

AURORA   It's okay, she can't see me.

Gudrun moves to Aurora, pulling her away.

GUDRUN   No, but this is ancient magic... Better to err on the side of caution, I think.

AURORA   This must be the day when...

Young Roland enters. He has escaped lessons and is on the run. Voices call after him from off.

DEVOIR *(from off)* Young sir!

Young Roland dashes over to young Aurora as she watches, curious.

YOUNG ROLAND Help me!

YOUNG AURORA What?

DEVOIR *(from off)* Roland!

YOUNG ROLAND I need to hide! Quickly!

YOUNG AURORA Alright, alright. Under here.

Young Aurora gestures to the cart, and young Roland quickly crawls underneath. Young Aurora tugs a cloth so it falls, concealing the Prince. Alfons Devoir, who is only an ordinary soldier at this point, enters and looks about for the Prince. He notices young Aurora and moves to her.

DEVOIR Rola— You there! What is your business here?

YOUNG AURORA Waiting for me Da.

DEVOIR And is this cart yours?

YOUNG AURORA Well, it's me Da's, yes.

DEVOIR You're the wool trader's daughter? Arne's girl? Aurora, isn't it?

YOUNG AURORA Yes, Sir. Da's talking to one of the Stewards about the delivery.

DEVOIR I see. Alright then. *(Beat)* Aurora, I don't suppose you've seen a little boy come this way, have you? About your age...?

YOUNG AURORA Sorry. Is he in trouble?

DEVOIR Oh no, I just need to find him, that's all.

YOUNG AURORA Oh. Well sorry.

DEVOIR Never mind. I'll keep on looking. He's going to get me in trouble, one of these days... Fare you well, Aurora.

YOUNG AURORA Goodbye.

Devoir goes. After a moment, young Roland speaks from under the cart.

YOUNG ROLAND Has he gone?

YOUNG AURORA Yes.

Young Roland crawls out, chuckling.

YOUNG ROLAND Silly Alfons. He never finds me!

YOUNG AURORA Why are you hiding from him?

YOUNG ROLAND He's supposed to make sure I go to lessons. But it's a sunny day and lessons are boring. So I ran away.

YOUNG AURORA Oh.

YOUNG ROLAND Thank you for your assistance, my Lady.

YOUNG AURORA I'm not a lady. I'm Aurora.

YOUNG ROLAND My lady Aurora then.

YOUNG AURORA If you're making fun of me, I'll smack you!

YOUNG ROLAND I wasn't!

YOUNG AURORA Hmmph.

UNFERTH   Blimey, a squirt and a vicious one to boot!

GUDRUN   Hush.

Young Aurora ignores young Roland and continues her spinning. The Prince watches her, curious.

YOUNG ROLAND What are you doing?

YOUNG AURORA Baking bread. What's it look like?

YOUNG ROLAND Honestly, I wasn't making fun of you. And thank you for helping me.

YOUNG AURORA You're welcome.

YOUNG ROLAND What are you doing? Really?

YOUNG AURORA Spinning thread.

YOUNG ROLAND Oh...

Roland watches her.

YOUNG AURORA What's your name?

YOUNG ROLAND I am Pr– My name's Roland.

YOUNG AURORA Do you live here?

YOUNG ROLAND Yes. Where do you live?

YOUNG AURORA With my Da on our farm, two days' ride from here.

YOUNG ROLAND What do you farm?

YOUNG AURORA Badgers.

YOUNG ROLAND Really?!

YOUNG AURORA Of course not! Sheep, obviously.

YOUNG ROLAND Oh, yes. Sorry.

YOUNG AURORA What do you do?

YOUNG ROLAND Oh, try and avoid lessons, mostly. How did you learn to do that?

YOUNG AURORA My Ma taught me. Before she...

YOUNG ROLAND I'm sorry.

YOUNG AURORA It's okay. Da says she's with her ancestors.

YOUNG ROLAND What does that mean?

YOUNG AURORA She was from a long way away, a land of warriors and trolls and wolves, where strange lights shimmer in the sky each night. That's what I was named for... In that land they believe your ancestors watch over you once they've passed on.

YOUNG ROLAND Sounds like an interesting place!

YOUNG AURORA Much more than here. I want to go there someday, I've had enough of spinning thread day after day.

YOUNG ROLAND Is it very difficult?

YOUNG AURORA Not really; this is the spindle, see. My Ma made this one for me. You twist it like this, and stretch out the wool...

As young Roland reaches out to touch the spindle, Devoir enters again.

DEVOIR   Prince Roland!

Young Roland leaps back guiltily. Aurora stares at him.

YOUNG AURORA Prince Roland?

YOUNG ROLAND Hello.

Young Aurora drops to one knee, perhaps a fist on heart; a pose she might have seen a soldier or her father do.

YOUNG AURORA I didn't mean to be rude.

YOUNG ROLAND No please, don't apologise. Please get up.

DEVOIR   Your Highness, I'm sorry, but your tutors are getting very... irate.

YOUNG ROLAND I'm sorry Alfons. I was just trying to enjoy the sunshine, and talking to Aurora, here.

DEVOIR   Yes, sir. But we really should go back in now.

YOUNG ROLAND Alright then. It was really good to meet you, Aurora.

YOUNG AURORA You didn't say you were the Prince.

YOUNG ROLAND No, I know. I'm sorry. But it was... Nice, to be just Roland for a little bit.

YOUNG AURORA If you weren't the Prince, I'd smack you for lying.

YOUNG ROLAND Will you come back again?

YOUNG AURORA I come with Da every couple of months.

YOUNG ROLAND I will look out for you.

YOUNG AURORA Okay.

DEVOIR Prince Roland...

YOUNG ROLAND Okay Alfons, I'm coming. Goodbye, Aurora.

YOUNG AURORA Goodbye, your Highness.

YOUNG ROLAND Roland, please.

Young Aurora looks nervously at Devoir.

YOUNG AURORA But...

YOUNG ROLAND It's alright; Alfons is a friend.

YOUNG AURORA Roland.

Young Roland smiles and he and Devoir leave. As they do the dream-vision fades and young Aurora and the cart disappear, leaving Aurora and her companions on stage. They begin to move on again.

UNFERTH So that was how you met him?

AURORA Yes.

GUDRUN Did you see him again after that?

AURORA Oh yes. He was always waiting when Da and I went to the castle. We'd talk and play... It didn't feel like we were a Prince and a poor farm girl, it just felt like...

GUDRUN Friends.

AURORA Yes.

UNFERTH So that's why you're doing this? Because you were friends?

AURORA Not just that...

UNFERTH What then?

AURORA I...

UNFERTH   What?

AURORA   I don't want to talk about it.

UNFERTH   I just think it's odd, you not wanting to say.

GUDRUN   You're hardly one to talk!

UNFERTH   What?

GUDRUN   Well, if you're so desperate for Aurora to spill her secrets, what about telling us how you lost your bridge?

UNFERTH   That's not the same–

GUDRUN   I mean, how do you lose a bridge?

UNFERTH   I didn't lose it, it was taken...

AURORA   Is it something to do with your fear of goats?

UNFERTH   I am not afraid of goats!

GUDRUN   What is it then?

UNFERTH   I just don't like them. Nasty, gruff, unpleasant things.

GUDRUN   But do they have something to do with how you lost your bridge?

UNFERTH   I don't want to talk about it.

December, November and July appear.

DECEMBER   Greetings Aurora.

JULY   And companions.

UNFERTH   You lot again?

GUDRUN   Don't be rude!

AURORA   Hello.

NOVEMBER   I must say you handled that situation with the siblings quite well.

AURORA   You were watching?

JULY   Well, we're observers, you see…

GUDRUN   And you didn't think you could perhaps lend a hand?

NOVEMBER   I'm afraid we can't, we're not allowed/ to…

GUDRUN   Not allowed to interfere. I remember.

AURORA   So why have you appeared now?

DECEMBER   Well, we thought we might wander along with you for a bit…

JULY   If you don't mind, of course?

AURORA   Of course not.

They move on. December and Aurora walk together.

DECEMBER   Yours was a strong friendship from the start, it seems.

AURORA   You saw that too?

DECEMBER   I know it must seem like we're snooping, but we're just…

AURORA   You care, don't you?

DECEMBER   Yes. We're supposed to be impartial, to stand above it all, but sometimes…

AURORA   It's not so easy.

DECEMBER   No. I'm sorry for what Oublier has done. I just wish…

AURORA   Yes?

DECEMBER   Nothing…

Dregil moves to Aurora, noses her hand to get her attention.

AURORA   Dregil? What's…?

DREGIL   Something is wrong here.

Dregil is alert, watchful. Aurora notices her surroundings properly. They have come to a village, mostly overrun by the Myrkwood, apparently empty. Aurora and her friends each become wary, alert.

AURORA   What is this place?

Cole whistles quietly.

UNFERTH   It's a village, apparently. Greenglade, so Cole says.

GUDRUN   But if this is a village, where are the people?

UNFERTH   They must have fled. Who'd stay here? The forest is taking over...

DREGIL   Stone-eyed troll...

UNFERTH   What does that mean?

DREGIL   The grass hasn't grown for more than a few days. And the thorns were being cut back till recently too, you can see the axe marks.

UNFERTH   Oh, alright clevernose!

AURORA   So people had stayed?

DREGIL   They're still here. We're being watched.

The group tenses, growing more alert. Just then a voice calls out.

VILLAGER ONE *(from off)* Alright, be off with you! We don't hold with bandits in Greenglade!

UNFERTH   Oi! Who you calling a bandit?

VILLAGER TWO *(from off)* Troll!

Two villagers enter, both armed with makeshift weapons. They're afraid but angry and move toward Unferth.

VILLAGER ONE What have you done to our village, monster?!

UNFERTH Me?

VILLAGER ONE Where have you taken them?!

VILLAGER TWO Where is my mother?!

UNFERTH They're mad.

GUDRUN Please, be calm.

AURORA What's happened here?

VILLAGER TWO Ask the monster!

UNFERTH Look, if you call me a monster once more I'll–

AURORA Be easy, Unferth.

December steps forward.

DECEMBER Good people, please!

NOVEMBER December!

JULY You mustn't!

DECEMBER These travellers have nothing to do with what has happened here.

VILLAGER ONE You're...

DECEMBER I am December.

VILLAGER TWO One of the Twelve?

DECEMBER Yes.

The two lower their weapons.

AURORA I'm sorry if we startled you, but... What has happened here?

VILLAGER ONE We don't know.

VILLAGER TWO We're the only ones left.

GUDRUN   Explain.

VILLAGER ONE   There's... Something out there. It's waiting in the shadows beyond the village.

VILLAGER TWO   We'd all decided to stay, in spite of Oublier and her threats and curses. We tried to carry on, cutting the thorns back...

VILLAGER ONE Then one day some people who'd gone out to fetch wood or water...

VILLAGER TWO They didn't come back.

VILLAGER ONE Others went to look for them, but...

AURORA   They didn't return either?

VILLAGER ONE That's how it's been for days. We're the only ones left now.

VILLAGER TWO Some people talked about a troll, heard strange noises in the wood.

VILLAGER ONE Toward the glade, some said. And then, when they went to look...

Aurora turns to December, July and November.

AURORA   Do you know what's happening?

DECEMBER I–

NOVEMBER December!

DECEMBER I'm sorry, Aurora.

Aurora looks at her companions. They nod in agreement, and she turns to the two villagers.

AURORA   Where is this glade?

VILLAGER ONE Not far... You're not going to go there?

GUDRUN   We might pass through...

UNFERTH   See what's going on, you know.

VILLAGER ONE But no one has come back!

AURORA   So we'll go and see why.

VILLAGER TWO I'll take you.

VILLAGER ONE You can't!

VILLAGER TWO Why not? My mother went out, and she didn't come back. Your brother did too. Don't you want to know what's happened to them?

VILLAGER ONE This is a bad idea...

UNFERTH   Oh, I expect so.

As they journey on, December, July and November hang back.

NOVEMBER What do you think you're doing?

DECEMBER I'm sorry!

NOVEMBER We cannot interfere!

DECEMBER I know. I know! But...

JULY   We are Guardians, December. We must let events follow their own course.

DECEMBER I'm sorry.

NOVEMBER Come on.

They rejoin the others, who journey through the forest. Soon enough they reach a clearing... It is filled with the people of the village, all turned to stone statues. At the centre of the glade a strange thing stands, something like the statue of a large troll-like creature, but seemingly made of iron...

AURORA   What is this place?

VILLAGER TWO Mother!

The Villager Two runs toward one of the statues, but Gudrun calls out.

GUDRUN   Don't touch it!

The villager pauses, obviously in two minds, and Aurora runs to them and stops them.

AURORA   She's right, look!

They all examine the stone villagers curiously.

VILLAGER TWO They're stone!

DREGIL   Petrified.

AURORA   This is strange magic.

UNFERTH   And it's not troll-work, I can tell you that much.

Dregil moves to the centre, sniffing at the Iron Troll.

AURORA   Dregil, what is it?

DREGIL   It smells... Wrong.

Villager One moves toward the Iron Troll as well.

VILLAGER ONE Looks wrong too.

UNFERTH   Doesn't look anything like a troll! More like an... iron soldier...

AURORA   That crest... It's the symbol of the Castle Guard!

GUDRUN   Wait! This creature... Its thread is human...

UNFERTH   It must have been enchanted by whats-her-face!

AURORA   Enchanted and set to turning people to stone!

DECEMBER Bravo!

AURORA   This... thing has done all this?

Perhaps a crack of thunder and Oublier appears.

OUBLIER Quite right, young lady.

AURORA Oublier!

OUBLIER Oh, it seems you know me, but I haven't had the pleasure...

AURORA I am Aurora.

OUBLIER I see.

AURORA Is this your doing?

OUBLIER Indeed it is. Do you like my little pet?

The Iron Troll begins to move, straightening up and turning to face Aurora.

AURORA Not really.

OUBLIER Oh, shame! Oh, I spy a birdie... Does that mean you're the ones who ruined my little joke with those three insolent young people?

DECEMBER Enough of this, Oublier!

OUBLIER December? You're not getting involved, are you? Isn't that against the rules...?

AURORA Leave her alone!

OUBLIER My my, we are a fierce one, aren't we? Very well then. I'll do no more... I'll let my pet do the work for me...

The Iron Troll moves to attack.

DREGIL Aurora, look out!

Dregil knocks Aurora out of the way as the Iron Troll swipes and misses. Gudrun leaps in and stops it with her own weapon.

GUDRUN Don't let it touch you, or you'll become stone– AAAH!

The Iron Troll moves, touching Gudrun and the Villagers. They cry out and stumble away, but before they have moved far they too have become stone.

UNFERTH   Right, now I'm angry!

Unferth moves to attack the Iron Troll.

OUBLIER   It's no use, child; you will never defeat the Captain...

UNFERTH   Captain?

AURORA   It's the Captain of the Castle Guard!

UNFERTH   That's lovely. Can I kill him now?

AURORA   No, wait!

Aurora leaps between Unferth and the Iron Troll.

UNFERTH   Aurora!

Aurora places her hand on the Iron Troll and calls out.

AURORA   Alfons Devoir!

The Iron Troll stops, and silence falls. Slowly there is a shimmering of magic, and the Iron Troll changes, becoming Captain Devoir, who collapses to his hands and knees. At the same time Gudrun and the villagers who were stone become flesh once more. Oublier is furious.

OUBLIER   How!?

AURORA   You seem to have a thing with names, Oublier. Why is that?

OUBLIER   Don't be so clever, little girl! You might interfere with my little games, but you will never lift the Prince's curse!

AURORA   Perhaps. But nothing you can say or do will stop me trying!

OUBLIER   Fool! You'll suffer for this! All of you will suffer!

Perhaps another crack of thunder as Oublier goes. Aurora moves to Gudrun, checks she is well, and then moves to Captain Devoir.

AURORA   Captain? Are you okay?

DEVOIR   I'm... I'll be alright.

AURORA   Why did she do that to you?

DEVOIR   I am the Captain of the Castle Guard, I have my duty... I would not abandon the Prince, even in his slumber... My lady, you freed me... I cannot thank you enough...

AURORA   My lady? Alfons, it's me... Don't you recognise me?

DEVOIR   Aurora? As the world turns, is it truly you?

AURORA   Hi.

DEVOIR   It's been so long! You were travelling far, seeking out your mother's homeland!

AURORA   I was, I did. And I've come back.

DEVOIR   Why?

AURORA   Roland... I have a debt to pay...

DEVOIR   I see.

The villagers have gathered about them.

VILLAGER   Lady Aurora...

AURORA   Are you all well?

VILLAGER   Well enough, my Lady.

AURORA   Please, I'm not... I'm just trying to help.

VILLAGER   And help you have. We cannot thank you enough.

VILLAGER   What will you do now?

AURORA   We go on. Perhaps Oublier was right, perhaps I cannot reach the castle, lift the curse... But I have to try.

DEVOIR   What can we do to aid you?

AURORA   You don't need to...

VILLAGER   You've saved us!

GUDRUN   We're just doing what we can.

AURORA   Please, return to your homes, your lives.

DEVOIR   Aurora is right. This is not a fight for an army, not now. Few can travel through the Myrkwood easier than many, and the way into the castle will not be achieved with numbers.

AURORA   Thank you.

DEVOIR   But if a time comes when you do need numbers, Aurora, send for us.

VILLAGER   We'll fight beside you.

VILLAGER   We promise.

AURORA   Thank you. Thank you all.

DEVOIR   Aurora, if you make it to the castle the gates are locked. Once I held the key, but Oublier took it from me when she turned me into that... creature... I do not know where it can now be found, but you will not make it into the castle without the iron key.

AURORA   Thank you, Captain.

UNFERTH   So much for a simple walk in the woods, eh Aurora?

AURORA   It's been a stranger journey than I'd first thought.

GUDRUN   Tales grow in the telling, you know.

DECEMBER   And your tale will grow more before it is done, I am sure...

Telling Tales

GUARDIANS   Telling tales so vast and free
The story grows through you and me
The adventure's not over, and soon you will see
That to end the story is your destiny
That to end the story is your destiny

As the tale grows ever onward
The threads of fate subside
The telling of the tale reveals
The ending you decide

Make the most of destiny
Make your tale sing true
If all of life's a story
Then this one belongs to you

The adventure's not over, and soon you will see
That to end the story is your destiny

Telling tales so vast and free
The story grows through you and me

End of Act One.

ACT TWO

The Guardians enter as the audience do, gather informally in their circle and talk together in small groups. December stands apart. As the lights go down they speak.

NOVEMBER Sister? What do you think of the story so far?

DECEMBER Oublier was... She was so angry. So cruel.

AUGUST Aye. She could not forgive what the people of the world had done.

DECEMBER Or what we had done.

APRIL Perhaps you are right.

DECEMBER It is a much larger tale than I had thought it would be.

JUNE But do not worry. For we have time...

JANUARY And there is more yet to be told.

AUGUST Unless...

FEBRUARY Do you wish to cry off, Sister?

NOVEMBER Will you tell another tale instead?

December considers for a moment.

DECEMBER Aurora doesn't turn back, does she?

MARCH That is part of the story...

DECEMBER No, she wouldn't turn back. Not even though the task was impossible.

MAY And so...?

DECEMBER I will continue the tale.

NOVEMBER Very well.

DECEMBER   So Aurora and her companions journeyed further into the Myrkwood, thinking on their encounter with the Lost One. They had met their enemy, it seemed, and her anger was great... Little did they know, however, that even at that moment Oublier's thoughts were turned towards them...

Oublier's stronghold. Some of her servants are there, strange, dark spirits of the Myrkwood, like dark dryads perhaps. Oublier storms in, furious.

OUBLIER   Curse them! Insolent, meddling wretches!

BRIAR   Something wrong, Mistress?

OUBLIER   Of course something is wrong, idiot! Someone is interfering!

SPIKE   Who?

OUBLIER   Some impudent girl-child and her companions. They've freed those three orphan brats and broken the Captain of the Guard's enchantment.

SPINE   Oh dear.

BARB   Did they get the iron key, Mistress?

OUBLIER   Of course not! That's hidden.

SPUR   Then what's the problem?

OUBLIER   The problem, nitwit, is that someone is trying to defy me! This girl is trying to reach the Prince to try and lift the curse.

SPUR   Ah.

OUBLIER   They won't succeed, I'll make sure of it! None can stop me! And yet... December was with them... She and my lost siblings are involved in this somehow, I know it!

SPINE   The Guardians of the Year?!

OUBLIER   They never accepted me. When the mortals
   cast me adrift I was left to rot, to be forgotten! So I took
   my revenge, but this Aurora and her companions, they
   all seek to interfere! I will make them all pay. I will be
   forgotten no longer...

Hidden Tears

OUBLIER   They've no idea what it's like
   To be the one who disappears
   In a crowd you're never seen
   Drowning alone in hidden tears

   The pain I feel within my heart
   Like shards of broken glass
   I'm the one that no one turns to
   That day must end, that time will pass

   Time to suffer for what they have done
   For endless dark they'll pay the price
   The forgotten sister will put things right
   As hidden tears turn into ice

   Incubuses
   Ettins
   Nymphs and Naiads
   Banshees
   Wraiths
   Hags and Dryads

   Hear my call
   Hear my plea
   Come and claim your destiny

   Incubuses
   Ettins
   Nymphs and Naiads
   Banshees

Wraiths
Hags and Dryads

Gather here, upon this dawn
Come and join the raging storm

OUBLIER Now my dark spirits, run and fly through the shadows! Find Aurora and her companions, and destroy them! Bring me their hearts! Go!

The host of dark spirits rushes off, and the scene shifts. We are in another part of the Myrkwood, and Aurora and her companions are journeying onward.

DECEMBER Meanwhile, in another part of the dark forest,

APRIL Aurora and her companions continued their journey.

AUGUST Deeper into the Myrkwood they travelled,

NOVEMBER until no sunlight penetrated the thorns.

AURORA This is a strange place...

UNFERTH Are we nearly there yet now?

GUDRUN Honestly, Unferth, you're like a child!

UNFERTH I'm only asking!

Dregil is suddenly alert, sensing something approaching.

AURORA We're closer Unferth, a lot closer.

DREGIL Something comes!

They look about warily. Aurora moves to Dregil.

AURORA What is it?

DREGIL I do not know. But it is not friendly...

The companions ready themselves for an attack, gathering in the centre, facing outward. There is a building of noise from off and then the dark host that Oublier summoned rushes on and surrounds them.

BRIAR	Here you are then!
SPIKE	The Mistress will be pleased!
AURORA	What do you want?
BARB	The Mistress is angry with you.
SPUR	You defied her.
SPINE	She wants your heart!
UNFERTH	What?
AURORA	Why?
BRIAR	Perhaps she is lonely.
SPIKE	Perhaps she is hungry!
SPINE	Who can say?
BARB	Ours is not to reason why...
SPUR	Ours is just to make you die!

The dark host attacks and the companions fight valiantly, but there are just too many...

UNFERTH	This is ridiculous!
GUDRUN	There's too many of them!
UNFERTH	For every one I squash it seems two more appear!
DREGIL	They are right, Aurora. We cannot win here.
AURORA	So what do we do?
GUDRUN	Perhaps discretion is the better part of valour.
UNFERTH	You mean we run for it?
GUDRUN	On this occasion it seems the best choice.

AURORA   Alright. Come on then!

Aurora and her companions flee, and the dark host follows them. It is a fighting retreat, and they cannot shake off their attackers. Suddenly they reach a clearing into which the dark host cannot follow them. Perhaps as some try to enter there are flashes of lightning, or some signs of magic.

AURORA   What's wrong with them?

UNFERTH   Ha! Had enough have you?!

DREGIL   They cannot follow us.

GUDRUN   Something holds them at bay...

AURORA   What is it?

GUDRUN   I don't know. Some art that's older than I am, Aurora...

Finally the dark host gives up and retreats.

SEPTEMBER As the strange dark host retreated, Aurora and her companions took in their surroundings.

DECEMBER   They stood before a small cottage,

MAY   almost smothered by the encroaching thorns of the Myrkwood...

Aurora and her companions enter. They approach the cottage warily, curiously...

GUDRUN   Do you know this place, Aurora?

AURORA   I don't think so... It seems...

DREGIL   Something is not right here.

UNFERTH   What is it?

DREGIL   I... cannot tell.

AURORA   I wonder if anyone lives here...

Aurora moves toward the cottage, and February, May and September move to stop her, becoming visible to the companions as they do.

FEBRUARY   You must stop!

SEPTEMBER You cannot proceed this way.

AURORA   Why not?

MAY   You must find another path.

GUDRUN   Tell us why?

DREGIL   Why did the Lost One's creatures retreat?

Silence.

AURORA   You won't lift a hand to help, but you'll hinder us when it suits you!

FEBRUARY   Things are not always as simple as they seem, young lady.

UNFERTH   Oh really?

DREGIL   Peace, Unferth.

UNFERTH   Oh come on! I mean, talk about stating the obvious!

GUDRUN   Be quiet, boulder-brain, you're not helping!

SEPTEMBER Please, Aurora, you should seek another road, and not disturb them...

GUDRUN   Them?

MAY   You should find another path.

AURORA   Who lives here?

FEBRUARY   They have suffered enough.

AURORA   I don't understand...

The Old Man and Old Woman emerge, curious at the commotion. They are surprised and then perhaps frightened by the strangers outside their home.

OLD MAN   Who's there? Why such noise?

AURORA   Please, don't be afraid!

DREGIL   We mean you no harm, old ones.

OLD MAN   A wolf! A wolf that talks!

UNFERTH   When it suits him to do so...

OLD WOMAN And a troll!

UNFERTH   Oh blimey, there's brains aplenty in this forest, isn't there?

OLD MAN   What do you want?

AURORA   My name is Aurora. These are my friends, Unferth, Gudrun, Dregil and the little bird is Cole. What are your names?

OLD MAN   I... don't know.

GUDRUN   Don't know?

The Old Man addresses February.

OLD MAN   But we know you, don't we...?

OLD WOMAN You keep the bad ones away...

FEBRUARY   That's right. And rest assured, you need not be afraid.

AURORA   How long have you been here?

The Old Man is confused by the question.

OLD MAN   Oh, some time, I think... The days pass so it's hard to know...

AURORA   And is there no one else?

This question clearly cause both the Old Man and Old Woman pain.

OLD WOMAN No... No longer. There was once, our little boy, but he is...

The Old Woman breaks down, weeping. Aurora moves to her, comforts her.

OLD MAN   She'll be right enough soon, my lady. Hurts, you see, 'cause we remember him a little, but can't...

GUDRUN   Can't what?

The Old Man shakes his head.

OLD MAN   Dearest pain locks up memory, dearest names unlock the truth.

AURORA   What does that mean?

OLD MAN   I don't know.

GUDRUN   Where is it from?

OLD MAN   Inside my head. Both our heads.

OLD WOMAN Dearest pain locks up memory, dearest names unlock the truth.

Dregil moves over to sit by the Old Woman, who strokes his head.

AURORA   Names again...?

GUDRUN   You think this is another of Oublier's cruelties?

AURORA   Perhaps. But what would she gain by tormenting these two?

Cole twitters.

UNFERTH   He says in his experience she doesn't need much of an excuse...

Aurora turns to May.

AURORA   What does this all mean?

UNFERTH   No good asking them.

The Old Woman has calmed now, and is stroking Dregil affectionately.

OLD WOMAN How beautiful your dog is! What is his name?

DREGIL   I am Dregil, my Lady, and I am no dog. I am a wolf.

The others are amazed at Dregil's behaviour.

GUDRUN   You're letting her stroke you.

UNFERTH   The last time someone who wasn't Aurora tried to do that you nearly bit his hand off.

AURORA   And why did you call her 'my Lady'?

DREGIL   She is not as she seems. Neither of them are.

AURORA   In what way?

GUDRUN   He's right. There's something... This is not where they belong...

Aurora confronts the three Guardians.

AURORA   You could tell me who they are, couldn't you? And what is wrong with them?

MAY   There are rules we cannot break, Aurora.

AURORA   Not even if it's the right thing to do?

Before the Guardians can respond or Aurora can say any more, the strange light and noise that signals the dream-visions starts again. The space begins to change as Aurora and her companions move aside to watch...

UNFERTH   Here we go again.

GUDRUN   Perhaps this dream will give us some answers?

UNFERTH   It can't be any less helpful than those three, at the least.

The space has transformed now, and it is the day before Prince Roland's 16th birthday, and the day that the curse will fall. We are in the Prince's new bedchamber; as he is turning 16 tomorrow he is moving from the rooms of his childhood into the Prince's royal chambers. Roland enters carrying a box of his things, followed by Devoir with another box.

DEVOIR   Is this the last of them, Sir?

ROLAND   Yes. Thanks, Alfons. You didn't need to help me, you know.

DEVOIR   Oh, old habits and all that.

ROLAND   But you're not just a soldier any more, someone of your rank shouldn't be carrying boxes about the place.

DEVOIR   If the Prince of the Realm can carry a box or two, surely the Captain of the Guard can as well?

ROLAND   I suppose so. I don't see why I have to move rooms anyway; I liked my old rooms.

DEVOIR   You've outgrown them, Sir. And it's traditional for the Prince to move into these chambers as he turns sixteen.

ROLAND   I suppose.

DEVOIR   So what's so special about these boxes then?

ROLAND   Nothing really. It's just stuff I've collected, gifts... Just...

DEVOIR   Precious things.

ROLAND   That's right.

Roland pulls a few things out of the boxes; a hawk's feather, a strange stone, the sorts of things we collect in childhood and cannot let go of... then he pauses, and slowly lifts out an old spindle. It is the one young Aurora was using before. Devoir sees it and tenses, concerned.

DEVOIR   What is that?

Roland holds it out to him. Devoir stiffens.

DEVOIR   Where did you get it?

ROLAND   It was Aurora's. She gave it to me...

DEVOIR   May I see it? Please?

Roland passes him the spindle, and he visibly relaxes.

DEVOIR   Sir, you shouldn't have this. The Lost One's curse...

ROLAND   Oh come now, don't be silly! It's just a spindle.

DEVOIR   If the King and Queen knew you had it...

ROLAND   It's not even sharp, Alfons! How am I supposed to prick my finger on it?

DEVOIR   But still...

ROLAND   Look, I don't use it, I just keep it. I look at it sometimes... Aurora gave it to me.

Pause. Devoir considers the spindle.

DEVOIR   She gave this to you...?

ROLAND   The day she left. She said she didn't have anything to compare to the gift I'd given her, but her mother had made it. I told her that made it too precious to give away, and she told me if I didn't accept it, she'd thump me.

DEVOIR   Ha! Sounds like Aurora...

ROLAND   She said she wouldn't need it on her travels, and perhaps it might remind me of her.

Pause. Devoir looks at Roland, speaks gently.

DEVOIR   It was a good thing you did, you know.

Roland shrugs.

ROLAND   It was important to her.

Pause.

ROLAND   Alfons... Do you think she is well?

DEVOIR   I am sure she is well, Roland. She's no doubt travelling far and having many adventures.

ROLAND   I wonder if she'll come back some day.

DEVOIR   I believe she will.

ROLAND   I'd like to hear about her journey, and the people she met on the way. Can I have the spindle?

Devoir is reluctant but hands back the spindle carefully. Roland takes it, runs a hand over it, tracing the shape.

ROLAND   To think something as simple as this is the beginning for so many things... Wool into threads, threads woven into cloth, and then clothing... And all from this—Ow!

Roland drops the spindle, clutches his hand... He has caught his finger on a splinter.

DEVOIR   Your highness!

ROLAND   It's nothing, Alfons, just a splinter. It's nothing...

Perhaps a crash of thunder as Oublier appears. December also appears, across the stage from Oublier.

OUBLIER   Nothing?! Oh, I'm afraid it is indeed something, little Prince!

ROLAND   Who are you?

OUBLIER   The last thing you will see in this life, brat!

DECEMBER   I'm sorry, Sister.

OUBLIER   December? You cannot stop me! Now, boy, die!

Roland staggers, fumbling to take hold of the spindle as the curse is overtaking him. As he collapses December is there to catch him. Gently she lays him down.

DECEMBER   It's okay. Sleep now, Roland.

Perhaps December places a hand to his forehead in blessing, and then stands, facing Oublier across his still form. Roland's breathing deepens as he falls into an enchanted slumber, his chest rising and falling. Outraged, Oublier stalks towards Roland; discovering he is clearly still alive, she is furious.

OUBLIER   What?! What trickery is this?!

The Guardians appear, coming to support December.

DECEMBER   No trickery, Sister! I had not laid my blessing on the Prince when you laid your curse.

APRIL   December has protected him.

OUBLIER   How dare you!

DECEMBER   He will sleep until an act of true devotion wakes him once more!

OUBLIER   Oh how poetic!

The Old Man and the Old Woman have been watching this with Aurora and her companions, but now they rush forward, into the vision. As they do so they change, becoming King Peter and Queen Melisende.

KING   Roland?!

QUEEN   My son! NO!

The King and Queen rush to Roland.

MAY   Fear not, he only slumbers...

OUBLIER   Only slumbers? Only? We shall see, brothers and sisters...

Devoir moves to stand between Roland and Oublier, sword drawn.

DEVOIR   You will not touch him!

Oublier makes a noise of annoyance and gestures, and Devoir is thrown across the room, landing in a crumpled heap.

OUBLIER   You'll regret that, Captain! But you are right, I will not touch him. I don't need to. Let the little Prince sleep; none shall ever get close enough to aid him!

Oublier throws her arms wide, and casts a spell; flashes of light, crashes of thunder, and perhaps the sound of thorns ripping through the earth. This is the sound we heard at the beginning, but now we are in the middle of it.

APRIL   Oublier!

AUGUST   What have you done?

OUBLIER   I have summoned the dark forest. The Myrkwood lies about this castle now, and it will grow outward with each passing day. None shall come close. None shall save the Prince.

QUEEN   No!

OUBLIER   More than this, I have bound his soul to the stones of this place; if you try and take him from this castle while he sleeps, then he will die!

KING   You cannot do this!

OUBLIER   You cannot stop me, little King!

QUEEN   You monster!

OUBLIER   HOLD YOUR TONGUE! I have had enough of your mewling!

KING   Please, Guardians, you must help us...

OUBLIER   They can do nothing. The ancient rules bind them. They won't interfere. And now, little King and Queen... What to do with you?

DECEMBER   Sister, please...

Oublier ignores December and moves to the King and Queen. They cannot move, bound by her magic, and she touches them both on the forehead.

OUBLIER   Dearest pain locks up memory, and dearest names shall unlock the truth.

The King and Queen collapse.

NOVEMBER   What have you done?!

OUBLIER   An exercise in irony, Brother. I don't expect you to understand... Goodbye. Make sure the Prince is comfortable, won't you. He'll be sleeping a while...

Oublier exits, laughing. The King and Queen begin to stir, and December and February move to them.

FEBRUARY   Your Majesties, are you well?

The King and Queen look puzzled, afraid.

DECEMBER   Your Highness, please say something.

QUEEN   Dearest pain locks up memory, dearest names unlock the truth...

Make a Memory

QUEEN   It's one thing to remember

KING   It's another to forget

QUEEN   When you open up your mind

KING   And find it full of regret

QUEEN   It eats away upon your heart

KING   I'll find the memory, go back to the start

BOTH   You've lost a feeling, once stirred inside of you
An echo of an angel, you know not what to do
Find forgotten dreams, that make us stand tall
Help me make a memory
Help me make a memory that can live in us all

QUEEN   It's gone, it's lost forever

KING   But what I cannot know

QUEEN   Rest your head upon my heart

KING   And feel its beating glow

QUEEN   I search within my fragile mind

KING   A memory lost, I cannot find

BOTH   You've lost a feeling, once stirred inside of you
An echo of an angel, you know not what to do
Find forgotten dreams, that make us stand tall
Help me make a memory
Help me make a memory that can live in us all

Help me, help me make a memory

The dream-vision fades and soon enough we are back in the Myrkwood. The King and Queen have become the Old Man and Old Woman again, and the Guardians are gathered about them. Aurora and her companions move back into the space. Aurora moves to the Old Woman, but it is clear she does not remember the vision.

AURORA   They're Roland's parents...

DREGIL   The King and Queen...

UNFERTH   That must be why they seemed so out of place. Hardly a fitting home for royalty, this old cottage.

DECEMBER   They could not bear to be far from their son.

FEBRUARY   December...

DECEMBER   What harm in telling them, February? It changes nothing! They have seen much of it already.

MARCH   Truly, it cannot hurt to tell them the rest, can it?

February sighs.

FEBRUARY   Very well.

AURORA   So... How did they come to this place?

DECEMBER   We brought them.

MARCH   The Prince could not be woken, however hard we tried, so he was laid upon his bed, still clutching the spindle.

AURORA   My spindle...

DECEMBER   There were two locks on the doors of the Prince's chambers, one of gold and one of silver.

SEPTEMBER   These were locked, sealing the Prince inside. We set what charms we could upon his chambers, to keep him safe.

JUNE   Oublier had summoned the Myrkwood, and the forest of thorns had grown about the castle walls, an almost impenetrable barrier.

MARCH   Many in the castle had fled in fear, and Captain Devoir gathered those who remained and led them out to safety, locking the front gates behind him.

JANUARY   We brought the King and Queen to this place; their memories are locked away, as you have seen, but something of them remains.

APRIL   They would go no further from the castle.

JULY   They would not leave their son entirely alone.

OCTOBER   But as Oublier had said, the Myrkwood began to grow.

MAY   With each passing day it spread further outward, and many of the people of this land fled their homes.

AUGUST   Oublier and the dark spirits who serve her wander the Myrkwood, tormenting those who remain.

NOVEMBER   So it has been for a long time, child.

AURORA   And the King and Queen... You can do nothing to restore them?

FEBRUARY   We cannot.

MARCH   The secret to their enchantment is beyond us.

AURORA   Dearest pain... Dearest names... Names again.

DREGIL   It seems to be a theme with her.

AURORA   Gudrun, can we free them as we freed Captain Devoir?

GUDRUN   I don't know.

UNFERTH   Can't hurt to try…

Aurora moves to the Old Man and places her hand gently on his forehead.

AURORA   King Peter Regale…

Nothing happens. Aurora tries with the Old Woman…

AURORA   Queen Melisende Regale…

Again nothing happens. The Guardians approach Aurora.

NOVEMBER Names will unlock the enchantment, you are right.

DECEMBER But we have not been able to discover what their 'dearest names' are.

AURORA   We cannot help them?

MAY   No.

NOVEMBER So we brought them here, watched over them.

DECEMBER And then you came.

AURORA   Roland is still there, in the castle?

JUNE   He sleeps, safe enough but out of reach.

AURORA   I just have to get to him.

DECEMBER Why, Aurora? What is it that is driving you on?

UNFERTH   I've asked her that, she's not telling.

AURORA   I… I have a debt I must repay.

UNFERTH   Oh, so if December asks you, you'll say! But when I ask, me who was the first to join you, it's just 'I don't want to talk about it!' That's charming that is.

GUDRUN   She was a lot more polite about it than you were.

DREGIL   But Aurora did not give much of an answer, even then, my friend.

UNFERTH   Hmmph. S'pose not.

MAY   Your course is set then, young lady.

AURORA   It is.

AUGUST   And you cannot be turned aside?

AURORA   I cannot.

FEBRUARY   Then... I wish you luck, Aurora.

DECEMBER   As do I.

OCTOBER   As do we all.

AURORA   Thank you. And thank you for telling me more of the story. I would ask one last piece of information, if I may...?

NOVEMBER   What is it?

AURORA   It is a long time since I left, and this Myrkwood has changed the land I knew so much... How much further is the castle?

UNFERTH   Are we nearly there yet?

Gudrun shakes her head in exasperation.

GUDRUN   Stone lummox.

AUGUST   Truly, you have not much further to go, Aurora.

FEBRUARY   The walls of the castle are close, though they are covered by the thorns of the Myrkwood.

NOVEMBER   The castle gates are a short way off, in that direction.

MAY   But they are locked, and I'm afraid the key is out of reach.

AURORA   Well, we've come this far. It would be foolish not to go a little further, don't you think?

The Old Woman moves to Aurora, and the Old Man follows her.

OLD WOMAN You're leaving.

AURORA   Yes. We are... Looking for someone.

OLD MAN   Someone lost?

AURORA   Yes.

OLD MAN   Lost things should be found, I think.

AURORA   I think so too.

The Old Woman lifts a silver chain from about her neck. From the chain hangs a silver key. She moves to the Old Man, and without speaking she lifts a gold chain from his neck. From the gold chain hangs a gold key. The Old Woman moves to Aurora and takes her hand. She holds it out and places the keys in it, closing Aurora's hand about them as she speaks.

OLD WOMAN Dearest pain locks up memory, dearest names unlock the truth.

AURORA   I don't understand...

OLD WOMAN Unlock.

Perhaps the Old Woman kisses Aurora's forehead, and then she takes the Old Man's hand and they go back into their cottage.

UNFERTH   Well that was a bit cryptic.

DREGIL   A key of silver, and a key of gold...

GUDRUN   To match the locks on the doors of the Prince's chamber...?

AURORA   Do they remember? Do they know I'm trying to free him?

GUDRUN   Perhaps some part of them does.

DREGIL   We should move on, Aurora.

AURORA   But what about the King and Queen?

FEBRUARY   There is little you can do for them, young lady.

Cole twitters.

UNFERTH   He says maybe they're like him? Maybe, if Oublier is defeated, their enchantment will break too.

AURORA   I hope so.

MARCH   We will guard them, Aurora, do not worry.

AURORA   Alright then. Let's go.

They journey on, and December goes with them.

AURORA   You're coming with us again?

DECEMBER   Sometimes it is not enough to simply observe a story. Sometimes you cannot help stepping into it.

AURORA   Whether you want to or not...

Aurora falls silent, distracted.

DECEMBER   What's wrong, Aurora? You seem... concerned.

AURORA   It was my fault.

DECEMBER   What do you mean?

AURORA   It was my spindle, the splinter came from it. The curse fell because I gave it to him.

DECEMBER   It isn't as simple as that.

AURORA   But it is, don't you see? If I hadn't given him the spindle Roland could never have fallen asleep! He'd be fine, the King and Queen would be well, the Myrkwood wouldn't be covering the land...

GUDRUN   Aurora–

AURORA   He gave me such a gift, and look how I repaid him!

DREGIL   Peace, Aurora. Be calm.

AURORA   How can I, Dregil? Look what I've done...

GUDRUN   It's alright, Aurora. I understand that you might feel responsible–

UNFERTH   Well I don't!

GUDRUN   Subtle as a rock, Unferth...

UNFERTH   Oh be quiet. I'm being serious. Aurora, did you want the Prince to be cursed?

AURORA   No!

UNFERTH   Did you give him that spindle to try and hurt him?

AURORA   No.

UNFERTH   Did you make sure the edges were rough precisely so that he'd get a splinter and fall into eternal slumber, dooming the kingdom to ruin?

AURORA   Don't be ridiculous, of course not! He was my friend, I gave him the spindle to remember me by, because I care about him. I never even thought of the curse! He's my friend.

Gudrun makes as though to move to Aurora, but Dregil stops her.

GUDRUN   Aurora–

DREGIL   Wait.

Unferth moves to Aurora, who looks up at him, hurt and angry. Unferth speaks softly, gently.

UNFERTH   You won't let me blame you, Aurora. Why then do you blame yourself?

Slowly Aurora realises the sense of Unferth's words. She hugs him.

AURORA   Thank you.

DREGIL   Bravo, Unferth.

Perhaps Gudrun hits him affectionately.

GUDRUN   Not bad, boulder-brain.

They move on, and arrive at the gates of the castle.

Is She the One? [Reprise]

GUARDIANS   Is this the time to look to the light?
You don't have to be strong to win the fight
Is she the one to make things right?
You don't need to be brave to do what's right
Can their friendship end this pain?
You don't need to laugh to stop yourself from crying
Will their trials bring an end to the rain?
You can still be a hero even with a fear of dying

Can I be the hero people want to see?
Can I find the strength hid inside of me?

AURORA   This is it.

UNFERTH   Finally! *(Beat)* Now what?

GUDRUN   Now we open the gates.

Gudrun pushes the gates, but they do not budge.

GUDRUN Locked.

AURORA As the Guardians told us... And we have no key.

UNFERTH Ha! Who needs a key when you've got a troll?

AURORA Unferth, I don't think–

UNFERTH Won't take me a mo...

Unferth stomps up to the gates and thumps them, but they still don't budge.

UNFERTH Hmmm.

He gathers himself, perhaps he take a short run-up, attempts to knock down the gates... but it is no use. Finally Unferth gives up, panting.

DECEMBER They are enchanted, good troll. Even such strength as yours cannot open them.

UNFERTH Now you tell me!

DREGIL Captain Devoir told us the same. We will not get into the castle without the iron key.

Unferth sits down, giving up.

GUDRUN So where's the key?

AURORA The Captain said Oublier took it from him. What would she have done with it...?

UNFERTH Maybe she keeps it with her?

AURORA Perhaps. But it doesn't feel right. She's malicious...

DECEMBER You're right. My sister would be more mischievous and cruel...

GUDRUN Like the King and Queen, hidden in plain sight, out of reach...

Cole twitters excitedly.

UNFERTH   What? Look, calm down, go slower! Up where?

AURORA   What's he saying?

UNFERTH   Some nonsense about looking but not seeing.

Exasperated, Cole flies up to the top of the canopy.

AURORA   Where's he going?

UNFERTH   Why am I supposed to know?

GUDRUN   Because you're the only one who can understand him!

UNFERTH   It's not my fault you lot can't speak bird is it!

AURORA   This isn't helping...

DREGIL   Look!

Whilst the others have been arguing, Cole has retrieved the iron key from its hiding place in the forest canopy above the gates. With a trill of triumph he flies back down to join Aurora and drops the iron key into her hands.

AURORA   The Iron Key!

GUDRUN   Where did you find it?

Cole twitters.

UNFERTH   He says it was up there, caught in the thorns above the gate.

AURORA   Hidden in plain sight!

UNFERTH   He said he tried to tell us, but we were so busy arguing he thought he should just go and get it himself.

DREGIL   A wise bird indeed.

AURORA   Thank you Cole!

UNFERTH   Yeah, not bad, pipsqueak!

GUDRUN   Well then, shall we see if it works?

Aurora moves to the gates and using the iron key unlocks them. The gates swing open and they move into the castle courtyard.

UNFERTH   We made it.

GUDRUN   We're not out of the woods yet, Unferth.

UNFERTH   At least we're in the castle though, eh?

Dregil approaches Aurora.

DREGIL   Aurora? Are you well?

AURORA   Hmmm? Oh, yes, sorry. I was just thinking... It's been a long time.

DREGIL   But you have returned.

AURORA   Yes...

The light and noise of a dream vision starts, but the space does not change this time; this vision occurs in the castle courtyard. Aurora and her companions move back to watch. Roland appears, perhaps sitting on a crate, waiting. He is facing away from Aurora.

UNFERTH   The Prince again...

GUDRUN   This must be before the curse fell.

AURORA   It is. This is...

DECEMBER   Aurora?

AURORA   This is the day I left.

GUDRUN   You're sure?

Aurora moves toward Roland slowly as she speaks.

AURORA   I'd come with Da for the usual delivery. It was just another day. He was waiting for me, as he always did, but he wasn't watching for me like normal. He was looking at something in his hands, and then when I got close–

Roland turns and sees Aurora. He grins at her.

ROLAND   Aurora!

Aurora and her friends are surprised; Roland can clearly see Aurora this time. She is playing her own part in this vision... Roland rises and moves towards her, growing concerned as she is reacting strangely.

ROLAND   What's wrong?

AURORA   Nothing, I just... It's nothing. Are you well, your Highness?

ROLAND   Aurora, come on, you know you don't need to call me that. It's just Roland, on today of all days.

Aurora smiles, settling into the memory now.

AURORA   Roland then.

ROLAND   Good.

AURORA   But why today of all days?

ROLAND   Because today is a special day.

AURORA   Why?

Roland just grins at her. Aurora glares at him.

AURORA   Roland...

ROLAND   Alright, alright! Today is a special day because I have something for you.

He holds out a letter to her.

AURORA   What's this?

ROLAND   Read it.

She opens the letter and reads.

AURORA   'Olaf Grimmrson, the young woman who has delivered this letter is Aurora Cherchant. Her father is a wool merchant and native to our kingdom, but her mother was born in your own homeland, a place Aurora has never seen. She is a strong, intelligent young woman, and would do well as an apprentice to you. I hereby ask that you give her leave to travel with you and discover the world beyond this kingdom...'

ROLAND   Aurora, are you...?

AURORA   Who is Olaf Grimmrson?

ROLAND   He is a merchant, trades in furs and iron... He comes from your mother's homeland. Alfons knows him well; he is a good man, and will take you with him.

AURORA   Why?

ROLAND   So you can see the land of your mother, and the world beyond it too.

AURORA   I can't leave. There's Da, and the farm, and...

ROLAND   Your father said it's okay.

AURORA   You asked him?

ROLAND   Before I spoke with Olaf. I think... I think he was pleased.

AURORA   Why have you done this?

ROLAND   You're my friend, Aurora. And I know how much you want to go.

Aurora is very still, and Roland begins to worry.

ROLAND   I wanted to give you something, because you've been my friend, and... I'm sorry I went behind

your back about it, but I thought you'd try to stop me, so...
Look, say something!

*Aurora makes a sudden move and Roland flinches, fearing
a thump... but she throws her arms about him and hugs him
tight.*

AURORA   Thank you.

ROLAND   You're not angry then?

Perhaps she hits him on the arm...

AURORA   Of course not, you idiot!

ROLAND   Hey!

AURORA   Thank you.

ROLAND   You're welcome.

AURORA   So... When does Grimmrson leave?

ROLAND   Tonight.

AURORA   What? But I don't have anything, I can't
just–

ROLAND   Your father brought it with him.

AURORA   You schemer!

ROLAND   Maybe...

AURORA   So... This means I won't see you again?

ROLAND   Not till you come back.

Aurora begins to look in her pack.

ROLAND   What are you doing?

AURORA   My Ma always told me that when friends
part ways for a long time, they give each other a gift.

ROLAND   You don't need to...

AURORA   Yes I do. Now close your eyes!

ROLAND   Aurora–

AURORA   Close them!

Roland does so.

AURORA   Hold out your hands.

Roland does so, and Aurora takes her spindle from her bag. She looks at it for a moment, then places it in Roland's outstretched hands.

AURORA   Open.

Roland opens his eyes and looks at the spindle. He gasps as he realises what it is.

ROLAND   Aurora, I can't take this...

AURORA   Course you can. Doesn't match up to your gift to me, but it's the best I can do.

ROLAND   But your Ma made this for you! That makes it more precious than anything I could give you! I can't accept it.

AURORA   You can and you will. And if you don't, I'll thump you.

ROLAND   Okay, okay! Thank you. I will take good care of it.

AURORA   I know you will. I suppose I had better go and find Da.

ROLAND   Yes. Olaf has rooms at the Wolf's Paw Inn; your father has taken your things there.

AURORA   Schemer.

ROLAND   I won't apologise.

AURORA   Good. Thank you.

ROLAND   Travel safe, Aurora. See the world. I just ask one thing though.

AURORA   What?

ROLAND   Come back someday. I'll miss seeing you.

AURORA   I'll come back, I promise.

The dream vision fades and Roland disappears. Aurora's companions gather about her.

AURORA   I promise...

GUDRUN   That was the debt you owed.

AURORA   He gave me a chance to see where Ma was from. Travel the world. Because of him I met all of you. So I had to come back, I had to try. I owe him.

DREGIL   As do we.

AURORA   What do you mean?

DREGIL   Because of Roland we met you.

UNFERTH   He's right.

GUDRUN   The Prince gave us a gift too.

UNFERTH   Shall we go wake him up to say thank you?

Aurora smiles at her friends, and they move into the castle together. Aurora and her companions move through the castle, heading for the Prince's chamber... Dregil speaks unheard words to Cole, and the Blackbird flies away.

Can I be the Hero?

AURORA   Can I be the hero people want to see?
    Can I find the strength hid inside of me?
    A single brave step began this epic trial
    Growing stronger day by day, mile after mile

    In friendship have I found, the ones to see me through?
    With courage, warmth and love they gave me hope anew

At trials end a friend in need lies peacefully in wait
I'll find the strength to change his cruel and hateful fate

Can I be the hero people want to see?
Can I find the strength hid inside of me?
A single brave step began this epic trial
Growing stronger day by day, mile after mile

She can be the hero

As the song ends, they reach the doors to the Prince's chambers. Gudrun pushes the doors, but they do not move.

GUDRUN   Locked.

UNFERTH   A lock of silver...

AURORA   And a lock of gold...

Aurora holds out the keys the Old Man and Old Woman gave her.

DREGIL   And two keys to match them.

AURORA   They must have known. Some part of them must have.

Aurora unlocks the doors and pushes them open. Slowly she moves into the room, her companions following. Roland lies on a bed at the centre of the space, sleeping. He lies peacefully, the spindle still clutched in one hand.

AURORA   Roland...

Aurora moves closer to the bed. She reaches out to touch the spindle.

UNFERTH   What are you waiting for then?

AURORA   What?

UNFERTH   Come on, kiss your boyfriend and wake him up.

AURORA	For the last time, Unferth, he's not my boyfriend.
UNFERTH	Okay, fine, whatever you say. Just get on with it!
AURORA	I'm not going to kiss him!
UNFERTH	Why not?
AURORA	I don't want to kiss him. He's my friend.
UNFERTH	But you have to break the curse!
AURORA	But he's my friend! It'd be weird!
GUDRUN	Who says kissing him's going to do anything?
UNFERTH	Shall I do it then?
ALL	No!
AURORA	Unferth, don't you dare!
UNFERTH	So what are you going to do?
AURORA	I... I don't know.

Sove Være Over Deg (Sleep be Upon You) [Reprise]

DECEMBER   That day won't be his last on earth
As sleep becomes his only notion
He'll lie at peace until the day
He's woken by an act of true devotion

AURORA	An act of devotion...
UNFERTH	I still think you should at least try kissing him...
GUDRUN	Oh, for pity's sake...
DREGIL	There are many ways to show devotion, my friend.

GUDRUN   Look, if you can't say anything helpful, don't say anything at all, alright?

Aurora sits on the edge of the bed, takes Roland's hand in hers.

AURORA   What do I do, Roland? I came back, like I promised. Back to a land where the beauty and balance of the world is sleeping, just as you are. I made it here, to you... What else can I do?

GUDRUN   Nothing, Aurora.

DECEMBER   You've been a true friend.

DREGIL   Devoted, even...

UNFERTH   Hang on... What if that's it?

GUDRUN   What did I just tell you?

UNFERTH   I'm serious. Dregil said it a minute ago; there are many ways to show devotion.

AURORA   What's your point?

UNFERTH   You heard your friend was in trouble, and so you came back across the sea and journeyed through an impenetrable, enchanted forest to try and help. If that's not devotion, what is?

DECEMBER   Well said, Stonebrother.

GUDRUN   You are full of surprises, you know.

UNFERTH   Oh, I was just saying, that was all...

AURORA   So if Unferth is right, what happens now?

DREGIL   Perhaps you should try and wake him up?

Aurora turns to Roland, as her companions wait with baited breath... she touches him on the shoulder, then shakes him slightly.

AURORA   Roland...

Perhaps Roland begins to stir.

GUDRUN   Look!

AURORA   Roland, it's me...

UNFERTH   It's working...

AURORA   Roland!

Roland wakes, slightly disoriented. Aurora helps him to sit up.

ROLAND   What's... Aurora?

AURORA   Hello.

Roland throws his arms about her.

ROLAND   You came back!

AURORA   I promised I would.

ROLAND   But, there was a splinter, and the Lost One, she came, and...

AURORA   I know. But it's done now. You're awake.

ROLAND   You came back to help me.

AURORA   What are friends for?

The other Guardians appear, entering the chamber in almost a formal procession. February guides the Old Man and Old Woman, who clearly don't recognise where they are.

AUGUST   Well done, young lady.

MAY   The curse is lifted.

MARCH   The Myrkwood will spread no further.

JULY   And in time it will wither.

UNFERTH   It's over then? That was a lot easier than I was expecting.

AURORA   No. It's not over.

UNFERTH   But the Prince is awake!

Aurora goes to the Old Woman, who smiles at her.

AURORA   But look, Unferth! They're still...

DECEMBER   You are right Aurora.

FEBRUARY   I'm afraid our sister's other enchantments remain...

Roland gets up and moves toward them.

ROLAND   What's happened to them?

AURORA   Roland... Do you know them?

ROLAND   Of course I do!

Roland takes a hand of the Old Man and the Old Woman in each of his.

ROLAND   Mum? Dad...?

Perhaps a sound of magic as the enchantment is lifted and the Old Man and Old Woman become the King and Queen once more.

KING   Roland...?

QUEEN   My son?

Roland and his parents embrace.

GUDRUN   Dearest pain locks up memory, dearest names unlock the truth.

AURORA   Dearest names... Mum and Dad.

Then the Queen sees Aurora, looks at her for a moment, puzzled.

QUEEN   Do I know you, young lady?

AURORA   Not exactly, your Highness.

ROLAND   Mother, this is Aurora, my truest friend. And these are...

AURORA   My companions. Dregil, Gudrun, Unferth, and—

She looks about for Cole.

AURORA   Where is Cole?

DREGIL   I asked him to do something for me.

UNFERTH   What?

DREGIL   You will see soon enough.

UNFERTH   You're as cryptic as this lot when you want to be, you know.

AURORA   But is Cole restored...?

DECEMBER   I'm afraid Oublier's other enchantments will remain as long as she does.

UNFERTH   I thought it was unlikely to be that easy.

A crack of thunder as Oublier appears.

OUBLIER   Oh, it will not be easy at all, believe me!

Aurora and her companions move to defend Roland and his parents.

UNFERTH   You again!

OUBLIER   Well obviously, who were you expecting?

DECEMBER   What do you want, Oublier?

OUBLIER   You keep out of this! So, child, you've woken the Prince, interfered in my plans again...

AURORA   I'm not afraid of you.

OUBLIER   Then I'll just have to change that, won't I?

DECEMBER   This has gone far enough, Oublier. You will torment this land no longer!

OUBLIER   Oh? Who's going to stop me? Not you, December, for the Guardians have their rules. Who's going to stop me?

AURORA   We will!

Aurora stands defiant, and her companions, Roland and the King and Queen stand with her. Oublier gives a contemptuous laugh.

OUBLIER   Seven? You really think you alone will be enough?

A Blackbird's call rings out as Cole flies back into the space, landing on Unferth's shoulder.

DREGIL   But we are not alone.

UNFERTH   Where have you been? ... What do you mean, 'reinforcements'?

DEVOIR *(from off)* Aurora!

Captain Devoir enters at the head of an army. Hunter, Grace and the Villagers are with him; all those Aurora and her friends have helped on their journey have come to aid them.

ROLAND   Alfons!

AURORA   How have you come here?

GRACE   Cole brought us word that you needed our aid.

AURORA   Dregil, you sent him to bring help?

DREGIL   It seemed prudent.

AURORA   So you see, Oublier, we do not stand alone.

HUNTER   And they never will.

OUBLIER   How touching. But ultimately futile. I will put an end to you all!

A cacophony of sound and light as Oublier casts a spell, and the Myrkwood about the castle changes, becoming a terrible dragon!

MARCH   The earth rumbled

OCTOBER   The very air shook

JULY   And the Myrkwood shifted

NOVEMBER   Moving and twisting

FEBRUARY   Weaving itself into an ancient and terrible
  shape

AUGUST   A fell serpent from the mists of legend...

UNFERTH   Well that's an eye opener and no mistake!

AURORA   Ready yourselves!

VILLAGER   But how do we fight that?!

ROLAND   All we can do is try.

AURORA   We stand together!

MAY   The dragon loomed over Aurora and her
  friends

JUNE   Lacerating claws

JANUARY   Ravening jaws

APRIL   Eyes glowing with malevolence

SEPTEMBER   Each wingbeat a hurricane

DECEMBER   And then...

December falters, perhaps realising what is to come. June comes to her, and takes her hand. Comforted, December takes a breath and speaks.

DECEMBER   Then battle began...

Battle rages. The dragon is fearsome and terrible, but Aurora and her army fight as best they can. Perhaps the

Guardians don't fight directly, but they assist in small ways, aiding people in dodging, etc. Aurora and Roland are side by side, and the dragon lunges at them, too fast for them to avoid.

DECEMBER   NO!

December can take no more, and leaps to push them out of the way. The dragon strikes her instead and she crumples.

JUNE   Sister!

NOVEMBER   December!

AURORA   No! What have you done!

Perhaps a lull in battle; the dragon retreats slightly as the Guardians gather about December.

OUBLIER   She should not have gotten involved, my brothers and sisters.

NOVEMBER   Perhaps not, Oublier.

AUGUST   But it was the right thing to do.

FEBRUARY   We see it now.

JANUARY   And we will put an end to this.

The battle rages again, and now the Guardians are aiding Aurora and her army. Slowly and surely they gain the upper hand. Finally the dragon is slain, and Oublier stands surrounded by the remaining Guardians. Working together, they weave their magick and bind Oublier.

OUBLIER   No! What are you doing?!

APRIL   What we must.

SEPTEMBER We bind you, Sister.

JULY   So that this world shall turn in safety.

MARCH   So its people may live in peace.

OCTOBER   We bind you.

FEBRUARY   And we banish you.

OUBLIER   NO!!!

Oublier vanishes. The dragon is slain. The survivors pick themselves up. As Oublier is defeated Cole's enchantment is lifted and he is reunited with his sister and brother. December lies at the centre of the stage, Aurora, Roland and Aurora's companions beside her. Perhaps Aurora cradles December in her arms.

AURORA   December... You sacrificed yourself for us. You shouldn't have done it...

DECEMBER   It was the right thing to do.

AURORA   But–

DECEMBER   Sometimes you cannot help stepping into the story. Farewell Aurora. It has been good to be a part of your adventure.

AURORA   No, you can't go!

DECEMBER   Don't worry. Perhaps we will meet again someday. But for now, farewell.

December dies.

AURORA   I don't understand... How can we meet again?

AUGUST   We are the Guardians of the Year.

NOVEMBER   We are eternal, though we are not immortal.

AURORA   What does that mean?

The Guardians do not reply.

UNFERTH   Oh, you're back to being cryptic again, are you?

FEBRUARY   I'm afraid the rules have not changed.

AUGUST   Though perhaps we've learnt that they can be... bent slightly, if needed.

GUDRUN   But this isn't one of those times?

SEPTEMBER Fare you well, Aurora.

MAY   We must leave you now.

AURORA   You will not stay and help us rebuild?

FEBRUARY   We cannot.

NOVEMBER   We must take our sister home.

ROLAND   We will honour her, always.

AURORA   Goodbye then.

GUARDIANS Farewell.

The world of the story fades, and the space becomes once more the place where the Guardians gather to tell their stories. The Guardians are the only ones left on stage now, gathered as they were about December.

JUNE   Are you well, Sister?

Slowly December gets up, perhaps helped by some of the others.

DECEMBER   It hurt, at the end.

FEBRUARY   The best stories often bring us pain as well as joy.

MARCH   In both the living and the telling.

JANUARY   So what now?

SEPTEMBER Is your tale truly done?

DECEMBER   Perhaps there is a little more to tell...

NOVEMBER   Then we listen, Sister.

DECEMBER   Oublier's work was undone, and the Myrkwood withered and died.

MARCH   The people began to return, and set about rebuilding.

JUNE   Aurora and her companions travelled the land

SEPTEMBER   And often Prince Roland journeyed with them

AUGUST   Doing all they could to aid the people.

DECEMBER   So it was that the darkness on the land was lifted, and the beauty and balance of the world was restored.

A sense of finality, the story December was telling has come to its close. The moment settles.

AUGUST   How do you feel now?

DECEMBER   I feel like I've lost something, but also...

JUNE   The last December?

OCTOBER   We all lost her, young one.

DECEMBER   But with the story... I found her again.

FEBRUARY   She lives on in the story.

DECEMBER   And in me.

A moment as they reflect on this idea.

NOVEMBER   It was a good tale.

APRIL   We thank you for the telling.

MARCH   But it hurt, you said. Do you regret it?

DECEMBER   The pain? No. Each step of our journey changes us, makes us who we are. I am December, and I do not regret the path I have taken or the tale I have told.

May approaches December, curious but also perhaps reluctant to speak.

MAY   What was it like, Sister? To die?

December thinks for moment, then smiles.

DECEMBER   What's it like to live?

Within Us All

This is the end
Our bitter sweet goodbye
This is the end

Our final curtain call
The stories told within these walls
Will live on, within us all

Stories that last a thousand years
Lifting spirits with joyful tears
This is the end
Our final curtain call
The stories told within these walls
Will live on, within us all

A wooden boy brought to life
A miserable scrooge full of strife
A flying boy in Neverland
An icy queen with an evil hand
A little girl with her magic sticks
Or an island full of pirates' tricks
A beast and a beauty who fell in love
Or a woodland hero free as the dove

These are the stories we could have told
Now it's time to tell your own
To show the world as stories end
That yours is the one to make amends

This is the end
Our bitter sweet goodbye

This is the end
Our final curtain call
The stories told within these walls
Will live on, within us all

Every story must come to an end
But don't despair
Just smile and share
As we take our final bow
The stories told will live in us all

This is the end
Our bitter sweet goodbye
This is the end
Our final curtain call
The stories told within these walls
Will live on, within us all

Perhaps during the song December is reunited with Aurora and her companions, as the story has come full circle... As the song finishes, focus shifts to December.

DECEMBER   I am December, and I have told my tale.

Lights fade down.

The End.

Rehearsal Images

Photos taken by Joshua Brierley (2017)

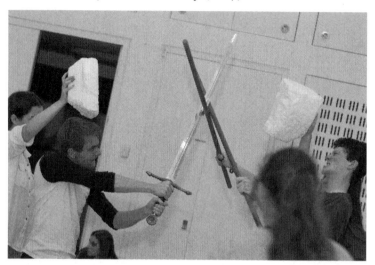

Aurora Metro Books

HAMLET adapted by Mark Norfolk
ISBN 978-1-911501-01-5   £9.99

COMBUSTION by Asif Khan
ISBN 978-1-911501-91-6   £9.99

DIARY OF A HOUNSLOW GIRL by Ambreen Razia
ISBN 978-0-9536757-9-1   £8.99

SPLIT/MIXED by Ery Nzaramba
ISBN 978-1-911501-97-8   £10.99

A GIRL WITH A BOOK by Nick Wood
ISBN 978-1-910798-61-4   £12.99

THE TROUBLE WITH ASIAN MEN by Sudha Bhuchar, Kristine Landon-Smith and Louise Wallinger
ISBN 978-1-906582-41-8   £8.99

SOUTHEAST ASIAN PLAYS eds. Cheryl Robson and Aubrey Mellor
ISBN 978-1-906582-86-9   £16.99

SIX PLAYS BY BLACK AND ASIAN WOMEN WRITERS ed. Kadija George
ISBN 978-0-9515877-2-0   £12.99

DURBAN DIALOGUES, INDIAN VOICE by Ashwin Singh
ISBN 978-1-906582-42-5   £15.99

WOMEN OF ASIA by Asa Palomera
ISBN 978-1-906582-94-4   £7.99

HARVEST by Manjula Padmanabhan
ISBN 978-0-9536757-7-7   £6.99

I HAVE BEFORE ME A REMARKABLE DOCUMENT by Sonja Linden
ISBN 978-0-9546912-3-3   £7.99

THE IRANIAN FEAST by Kevin Dyer
ISBN 978-1-910798-93-5   £8.99

NEW SOUTH AFRICAN PLAYS ed. Charles J. Fourie
ISBN 978-0-9542330-1-3   £11. 99

BLACK AND ASIAN PLAYS Anthology introduced by Afia Nkrumah
ISBN 978-0-9536757-4-6   £12. 99

www.aurorametro.com